# of Vincennes

Patriot Kids of the
American Revolution Series

Book Three

To Justin,

GEOFF BAGGETT

Cocked Hat Publishing
P.O. Box 2382
Cadiz, Kentucky 42211

ISBN: 0-9973833-6-4
ISBN-13: 978-0-9973833-6-2

DEDICATION

To all of the brave boys and girls who lived on the Colonial-American frontier. It is because of their courage and sacrifice that we enjoy the great nation that we have today. We must strive to find new and creative ways to honor their memories.

Cover Design by Natasha Snow - natashasnow.com

BOOKS FOR KIDS BY GEOFF BAGGETT

Patriot Kids of the American Revolution Series

Little Hornet (Book One)

Little Warrior (Book Two)

Little Spy of Vincennes (Book Three)

Kentucky Frontier Adventures

A Bucket Full of Courage: Betsy Johnson of Bryan Station

A FORGOTTEN PLACE IN THE AMERICAN REVOLUTION

In the early 1700's the vast "Northwest Territories" of Colonial America, known as the "Illinois Country," stretched across the modern states of Indiana and Illinois. The first Europeans to settle in this region were the French. They established farming and hunting villages near the many rivers that flowed through the region. For the most part, these Frenchmen lived in peace among the Native Americans in the region.

After the end of the French and Indian War (1763), the British took control of the Illinois Country and established several outposts and forts for their army. They used the area as a "base of operations" to launch attacks against frontier outposts in Kentucky. An American colonel from Virginia, George Rogers Clark, wanted to end the attacks and the British influence upon the natives in the Illinois Country. He led an army to invade the region in 1778.

This book tells about this invasion from the perspective of some of the French settlers who lived in the tiny village of Vincennes (now in Indiana). It deals with several difficult themes. You will read about the war, violence, guns, and Native Americans (called Indians or "Injuns" in the 18th Century). If you have questions about these things, I encourage you to talk to a parent or another responsible adult in your life. Ask questions. Learn more about your history. If you have difficulty with any of the unique "Revolutionary War words" that you encounter, be sure to check out the glossary in the back of the book.

Geoff Baggett

Part I

Revolution!

CHAPTER ONE
A SECRET TUNNEL

February 18, 1778
Vincennes
A Remote French Village on the Northwest Frontier

The four boys heard a dull, crunching sound from deep inside the tunnel. A cloudy puff of dust drifted out of the opening. The odd sound was accompanied by a brief scream of fear. Then they heard a frantic call echo from deep inside the tunnel. "Help! Pierre! Jean-Luc! Please help me! I am buried!" The invisible voice screeched and screamed without ceasing from the darkness of the cavern.

That desperate voice belonged to their tunnel-digging friend, Gaspard Turpin. It launched Pierre Grimard and the other diggers into immediate action.

"Quickly! We must pull him out!" urged Pierre.

He and the other three boys each dropped their buckets full of dirt and grabbed the rope that was dangling from the tunnel opening. It was their "safety rope," and it was always tied to the ankle of the boy who was digging at the far end of their hidden tunnel. The boys had never needed to use the rope before, but now it seemed that their luck had finally run out.

The frightened, frantic boys pulled with all their might. They were desperate to rescue their friend out of the dark hole. They tugged and strained and grunted, but Gaspard would not budge. He was a very tiny fellow. The four strong eight-year-old boys should have been able to pull him out with ease. Something was horribly wrong.

"Pull harder!" squealed Pierre. "The sides have collapsed on him! Gaspard could die!"

The desperate boys strained against the enormously heavy weight at the other end of the rope. Soon they felt the tiniest bit of movement. The rope then began to wiggle and vibrate as Gaspard kicked his leg.

Pierre hissed, "I think he may be loose! Pull again! Quickly! We must save our friend!"

Though the situation was urgent and Gaspard was in much danger, Pierre attempted to keep his voice as quiet as possible. He did not want to alert the British soldiers who stood watch atop the walls of nearby

Fort Sackville. They definitely did not want to get caught by the ill-tempered, suspicious Redcoats.

The boys were actually digging inside an abandoned shack. It served as their club and hideout. The old building sat hidden in a thick cluster of woods beside the Wabash River, a mere thirty feet from the nearest wall of the fort. It was surrounded by tall bushes and covered with vines. No one from Vincennes but these five little boys even knew that the shack existed. It was their secret hiding place. It was their wonderland of fun and imagination.

The boys had been working on their underground tunnel for just a little over a month. Their goal was simple. The devious little troublemakers wanted to dig their way beneath the walls of Fort Sackville so that they might "borrow" a few supplies from the "enemy" army. They also wanted to play some tricks and jokes on the unsuspecting British soldiers and cause as much mischief as possible. It would be utterly heartbreaking if the British discovered their little spy game before they were finished.

The boys did not fully understand it, but the game they were playing was a very dangerous one, indeed. Fort Sackville was the command post of the British Army in the region around Vincennes, and that army was currently at war with the rebel Americans of the United States. The Americans called the war a "revolution." Because of this ongoing conflict, the British did not trust anyone, not even their longtime

French neighbors. They worried constantly about an invasion by the Americans who lived down south in the wild Indian lands of Kentucky. They worried, also, about a possible rebellion among some of the local French people.

The little fur-trading and farming village of Vincennes had always been a French community. French explorers and settlers from Canada founded the village around the year 1700. But now the entire area officially belonged to the British. It was English land. They took a vast amount of American territory from France after winning the French and Indian War in 1763. The British controlled every one of the tiny French villages and settlements in the region. Their authority reached westward all the way to the mighty Mississippi River.

There were several dozen British soldiers stationed at Fort Sackville. The commander of the fort was a likable fellow named Lieutenant Governor Edward Abbott. The governor was generous toward the local residents and respected by the men of Vincennes. But the kindly Governor Abbott would not respond favorably to a secret tunnel beneath his fort. If the boys were ever caught they would be in very serious trouble. It could even cause problems for their fathers. All of their dads served in the Vincennes militia under Governor Abbott's command.

Of course, the mischievous little boys did not worry about such grown-up things. They just wanted to have some fun, and digging a secret tunnel was the ultimate adventure!

But their current disaster was no fun, at all. Gaspard was caught beneath a mound of collapsed earth. He might be injured. He could even die! Pierre and the other boys were frantic with worry as they continued to pull with all their might on the rough rope. They felt the weight of Gaspard's body moving steadily in their direction. Soon the boy's black shoe and white sock came into view at the entrance of the tunnel.

Pierre dropped the rope and grabbed his friend's leg. He grunted as he gave it a mighty tug. The other boys continued to pull the rope. Gaspard popped out of the tunnel and landed on his belly on top of a pile of soft dirt. Pierre and the other three boys fell backwards with a loud thud and landed in a messy heap on top of one another. Poor Gaspard lay still and silent. His entire body and head were covered with loose dirt.

Pierre climbed off of the pile of fallen boys and darted toward his buddy. He shook the boy's shoulder. "Gaspard! Gaspard, my friend! Speak to me!" Jean-Luc, Adrien, and Quentin scrambled to their feet and joined Pierre at the injured boy's side.

Gaspard did not respond. Pierre grabbed his arm and flipped him over onto his back. The boy's eyes were closed. His face and neck were streaked and stained black from the dark soil of the tunnel. He did not move. He did not even appear to be breathing. Pierre's heart skipped a beat. He thought for certain that his friend was dead. He wondered how he would ever explain this tragedy to his father. Then he imagined the heartbreak of Gaspard's parents, Francois and Josephine Turpin.

Pierre shook his head and cleared those horrible, dark thoughts of death from his mind. He reached down and gave Gaspard a vigorous slap across his cheek. Still, the boy did not move. Pierre leaned close to the injured boy's face and screamed, "Gaspard! Wake up! Now!"

Quite unexpectedly Gaspard's eyes popped open. The whites of his eyes glowed brightly against his gray, dirt-stained skin. Then his mouth expanded into a wide smile, revealing his shiny white teeth.

"Hello, Pierre," he mumbled. He coughed and spit some dirt out of his mouth. "What took you fellows so long?"

Pierre and the other boys collapsed onto the cold ground beside Gaspard. They each breathed huge sighs of relief. They shook Gaspard good-naturedly and punched his shoulder in feigned anger. But really, deep down, they were so very glad that their friend was alive.

Pierre slapped Gaspard across his belly and then scolded him, "We thought you were dead for sure! We pulled and pulled but you would not budge."

"I couldn't move, Pierre! I had a mountain of dirt and rocks on top of me!"

"What happened?" Pierre demanded. "What caused the cave-in?"

"I don't know. I was digging and making really good progress when the right side of the tunnel suddenly let go and collapsed right on top of me. It snuffed out my candle immediately and everything became pitch-black dark!"

"How much of the right side collapsed?" asked Pierre.

"I'm not sure. Maybe a few feet. It covered me from my neck to my knees. It scared me really badly. I had only a very small pocket of air beside my head. I yelled for you fellows, but wasn't sure if you could hear me."

"Oh, we heard you," responded Pierre.

"Yes! It sounded like a whole barn full of roosters was buried in that hole with you," teased Quentin, chuckling. The boys giggled and quietly mimicked his frantic cries from the depths of the tunnel.

"I guess I was yelling quite a bit, wasn't I?" Gaspard grinned again. "I knew you fellows heard me, though, when I felt the rope tightening against my leg. When the tugging started I thought you boys were going to pull my leg off! It took me a while to wiggle and move around so I could get some of the dirt off of my back and work myself free."

"Well, we got you out. That's the important thing," declared Pierre, smiling broadly. "There will be no funeral in Vincennes tomorrow. Your mother will be very happy." He slapped his friend on the shoulder. "Come, now. We must get you cleaned up. You cannot go home looking like this. We don't want any extra attention or nosy questions from our parents."

For the next half hour the boys helped Gaspard shake and clean the dirt from his clothing. The poor lad had dirt everywhere. It was in his shoes, in the pockets of his weskit, and even inside of his socks. He had to remove every single item of clothing, turn all of his garments inside out, and shake them thoroughly.

Jean-Luc fetched Gaspard a fresh pail of water from the Wabash River. The frigid river water was all they had available for washing.

Gaspard stuck his hand into the bucket and quickly jerked it back out. The water was so cold that he gasped. He shook his head. He whined, "No, guys! That's too cold. Can't we build a fire and warm the water?"

Jean-Luc shook his head. "Certainly not! We would be discovered for sure and all of our plans would be ruined."

"I think our plans are already ruined," answered Gaspard. "I don't think we can ever finish that tunnel. I know that I will never go back into that hole again."

"You're probably right. But we can worry about all of that tomorrow. Right now you need to get washed before you go home," answered Jean-Luc.

"Look at it this way. At least you don't have to sit in the water," encouraged Adrien, grinning from ear to ear as he sloshed the frigid water inside the bucket.

Gaspard frowned, poked out his bottom lip, and muttered, "That's easy for you to say."

"Well … get on with it," urged Pierre. "It will be dark soon, and I'm tired of staring at your pale legs. I swear! They are whiter than a baby's diaper!"

The other boys snickered and laughed.

"Yes, hurry up!" urged Jean-Luc. "Mama will have supper ready soon."

Gaspard reluctantly grabbed an old piece of cloth that hung on a nail sticking out of a nearby post. He plunged the rag into the water, took a deep breath, and then began to scrub. It was freezing cold, so he worked quickly. His skin turned a pale blue color and his teeth began to chatter. Once he was reasonably clean his buddies helped him get dressed and then wrapped an old wool blanket around him.

The temperature was dropping quickly with the approach of sunset, so Pierre grabbed a large piece of discarded canvas from the corner of the shack. He shook the dust out of the ancient cloth and declared,

"Boys, let's all get under this and help Gaspard get warm."

The five boys sat on the ground and leaned back against the only solid wall that remained in the old, abandoned shack. They scooted close to one another and covered up together beneath the huge piece of canvas. After a few minutes Gaspard's teeth stopped chattering. It was quite warm with all five boys wrapped up inside the thick cloth.

The five friends sat quietly and comfortably and waited for the sun to go down. As darkness descended upon the inside of the shack the cloudy sky outside changed to a dark shade of purple. They could see the pink light of the descending sun glistening on top of the waters of the Wabash. It was a beautiful sunset, and a good ending to a fun day.

Gaspard declared quietly, "I am truly thankful that you guys got me out of that hole. You saved my life."

"That's what pals do," declared Pierre. "And we are all pals, aren't we?"

From the darkness inside the old shack the friendly voices of the other four boys responded in unison with a single word of affection. "Pals."

CHAPTER TWO
FROGS AND TALL STRANGERS

Five Months Later - July 20, 1778

The boys gave up their tunnel-digging endeavors soon after Governor Abbott and the entire garrison of British soldiers departed for Fort Detroit early in the month of March. The British left the fort under the command of Captain Francois Bousseron, the owner of the local general store and the commander of the French militia. With the British gone the notion of digging under the wall became much less intriguing. None of the boys wanted to dig their way into a fort that their own fathers occupied.

It was Monday morning. Pierre Grimard, Sr., was preparing to go to the roll call and muster of the militia at Fort Sackville. He sat outside on the front porch of the Grimard home and quickly polished his rifle with an oily cloth. He was growing impatient with his oldest son, who also happened to be named Pierre. It had been several minutes since he sent the boy inside to get his hat and leather belt. It was taking entirely too long, and the elder Pierre did not want to be late.

Inside the house little Pierre searched frantically. The boy was frustrated. No matter how hard he tried he could not find his papa's belt.

"Where is it?" he wondered out loud. "I know it is somewhere in this house!"

It was a frustrating mystery. Pierre found the hat easily enough. It was hanging on the back of a chair beside the fireplace. But the belt seemed to have disappeared. He had already searched all of the usual places. The belt was not in his papa's trunk, which was where he customarily stored it. It was not under the bed or hanging over the fireplace.

Pierre was getting worried. His father could not report for militia duty without his belt. That dark brown leather strap held his papa's hunting knife, two leather shooting pouches, and his fearsome Indian tomahawk. There was no way that he could stand guard at the fort or go on patrol without his fighting equipment. So, little Pierre kept searching. The longer he looked, the more worried and annoyed he became.

Once again, he heard his papa's irritated voice calling from the front porch. "Pierre! Son! Hurry up! Bring my belt and hat now! I am in a hurry!" Then he heard his father declare to his mother, "I swear, woman, your son moves as slowly as the backwaters of the Wabash River."

Little Pierre grinned when he heard his mother chuckle and reply, "The boy moves about as quickly as you do when there is some actual work to be accomplished."

Pierre's mother, Genevieve, was a spunky little woman. In addition to Pierre, she had two other sons to keep up with. Jean-Baptiste was almost five years old. Then there was the baby brother of the family, a rowdy and adventurous little boy named Charles. He was three years old and always wandering off and getting into trouble.

Parenting three little boys in the wilderness was a very difficult, full-time job. Pierre had recently heard his parents trading whispers during the night about a baby. He suspected that his mother was expecting another child. The thought of another baby in the house made Pierre smile. He hoped that this one might be a girl. He longed for a quiet, calm baby sister.

Pierre was just about to give up his search when he spied the handle of his papa's tomahawk peeking from behind his wool winter coat. The heavy coat hung on a nail beside his parents' bed. He removed the huge coat from its nail and tossed it onto the bed, revealing the leather belt with its knife and tomahawk hidden underneath.

He screeched in victory, "Whoopee!" He grabbed the belt and sprinted toward the front door. He was sweaty and red-faced when he emerged onto the porch.

"Here I am, Papa! I had a horrible time finding your belt."

"It was in my trunk, where I always keep it," responded his father, sounding annoyed.

"No, it wasn't, Papa! I looked there first. I finally found it hanging on the nail beneath your winter coat."

"Oh!" responded Pierre. "I don't remember hanging it there. Most strange ..."

"You did not put it there, husband. You left the horrid thing dangling on the back of one of my dining chairs. I accidentally knocked it off one day last week and that gruesome hunting knife popped out of its sheath and almost sliced off my toes." She shuddered as she remembered the moment of the accident. "I hung it safely beneath your winter coat so that Jean-Baptiste and Charles could not reach it."

"Thank you, my dear."

"You are quite welcome. You should try putting things in their proper place from now on."

"Yes, Mama," the elder Pierre replied, rolling his eyes at his son. Little Pierre covered his mouth and choked back a giggle.

"I saw that!" snapped Genevieve. "I think you had better get to the fort before they hang you for mutiny, or before I spank you for making a mess of my house." She smiled warmly.

Pierre winked at his wife as he strapped his belt around his waist. He tucked his hunting knife inside the belt on his left side and inserted the handle of his tomahawk on the right. He grabbed his rifle off of the table and popped his cocked hat sportily onto his head. As he shuffled down the porch steps he called over his shoulder, "Woman, I'll be home at noontime for dinner."

"See that you are," she called back. "And do not be late!"

Pierre exited the gate and then marched steadily up the street from his house toward Fort Sackville.

Little Pierre grabbed his own hat from a stool on the porch and took off running toward the gate.

"Where are you going, young man?" demanded his mother.

"I am going to find Gaspard and Jean-Luc. We were thinking about trying to catch some frogs at the pond."

"That sounds good. Some fried frog legs would be a treat. But do not get into the water with your clothes. And see to it that you are home when your father returns for his dinner."

"Of course, Mama."

"Come and kiss your mother before you go."

Pierre darted onto the porch and kissed his mother's cheek. "I love you, Mama."

"I love you, too, Pierre. Have fun, but be careful."

The frog hunt was not going very well. In just over three hours the boys had only captured two medium-sized amphibians. It was not even close to being enough to provide a good meal of tasty fried frog legs. The three boys lounged in the shade beneath a huge willow tree and stared at their two puny frogs as the critters swam in endless circles inside their wooden bucket. The bored lads chatted, chewed on long blades of sweet grass, and tossed pebbles into the shallow pond. Despite the warnings from their mothers, all three boys were thoroughly soaked with pond water.

"We need to make a net for gathering frogs," declared Gaspard. "It's simply too difficult to capture them with our hands. They're too slippery!"

"Or gigs, perhaps," added Pierre. "Papa told me about them. They are like spears that have little forks on the end. They are for sticking frogs."

"Ugh!" wailed Gaspard. "That sounds nasty! Frog guts will get everywhere! I don't want to poke them. I just want to catch them."

"Well, Gaspard, our mothers have to poke them before they skin them and prepare their juicy legs for supper. We could simply save them the trouble," responded Pierre.

Gaspard shrugged. "I suppose. Maybe your papa can show us how to make some frog spears."

"Frog gigs," corrected Pierre.

Jean-Luc, who had been unusually quiet for most of the morning, interrupted their frog hunting conversation with a very strange question. "Do either of you fellows know what a Virginian is?"

Pierre and Gaspard stared at their friend with looks of confusion.

"I have never heard that word," declared Pierre, shaking his head.

"Neither have I. It sounds strange. Is it some kind of animal?" asked Gaspard. "Like an elk or a buffalo? Or a panther, perhaps?"

"I don't think so," responded Jean-Luc. "They sound very scary, whatever they are. I heard my mother talking about them with Mrs. Descoteaux. She told Mama that Virginians have arrived in Illinois and that they have taken over all of the French towns to the west along the Mississippi River." He paused and then gave his friends a very serious, frightened stare. "She said that she heard the Virginians are killing all of the men and eating the French children."

Pierre laughed out loud. "That is the dumbest thing that I have ever heard! You can't believe a word that crazy old woman says. You know how she likes to spread gossip and lies. Nothing eats children … except for bears, maybe."

"Her story does sound a bit silly," echoed Gaspard.

"But it still makes you wonder, doesn't it?" challenged Jean-Luc. "What could a Virginian be? I don't know whether to be curious or frightened."

"Well, no matter what they are, our fathers will not allow them to harm our families or our homes," promised Pierre.

The other two boys nodded and grunted in agreement.

"Good," declared Pierre, slapping his hands on his knees. "Enough of this talk about Virginians. I'm hungry. Mama and Mrs. Turpin are cooking a huge meal for our fathers today. They should be home from the fort very soon. Shall we go to my house and get some dinner?"

"I can't. I have to go to Bousseron's store and fetch some salt pork and sugar for my mother," replied Jean-Luc as he stood and knocked the grass and dust from his breeches. "But you fellows go ahead. I will get my dinner at home and then meet you back here this afternoon."

Gaspard proclaimed hopefully, "Maybe we can do a better job at catching these frogs."

Jean-Luc chuckled and waved as he ran across the meadow toward his home.

Pierre grinned at Gaspard. "Let's go get that food."

Gaspard slapped his friend on the knee and shouted, "Race ya!" Both boys jumped to their feet and sprinted around the pond as they raced toward Pierre's house.

❧

"Leave something for your fathers!" scolded Josephine Turpin. "You boys act as though you haven't had a meal for a week!"

Pierre and Gaspard laughed at the good-natured teasing from Gaspard's mother. Though she scolded them and sounded displeased, both boys knew that she was very proud of the growing boys and their hearty appetites. The lads smacked their lips and savored every bite of the tasty stew and fresh bread.

"This beef stew is wonderful, Mrs. Turpin," Pierre declared, slurping from his spoon.

"It certainly is, Mama!" affirmed Gaspard. He burped loudly. "Is there any fruit?"

His mother shot him a look of disgust and pointed her finger in shame. "I have taught you better manners than that, Gaspard Turpin!" She winked at her son. "There is some sliced melon in the house. You boys can each help yourself to a piece."

Pierre and Gaspard ran inside and grabbed a slice of sweet, pink watermelon. They sucked on the juicy melon as they walked down the stairs from the porch. Moments later they spied several men of the militia walking along the dusty road. Both boys ran to meet their fathers.

"Papa! Papa!" exclaimed Gaspard. "Mama has been working with Mrs. Grimard to prepare a huge meal for you. It is delicious!"

"I hope you saved me some," teased Francois.

Gaspard teased him back, "There's a little bit left."

Each boy took his father by the hand and escorted him to the bountiful table prepared in front of the Grimard house. There was a large pot of beef stew, a platter stacked high with steaming loaves of fluffy bread, and several bowls of fresh garden vegetables. Cold water and hot tea were available to wash down the hearty food.

"Gaspard and I have already eaten our dinner, Papa. Will it be all right if we go and play?" begged little Pierre.

Pierre glanced at Francois, who nodded his assent. He answered, "Of course boys. Have fun, do not wander too far, and stay out of trouble."

"Yes, Papa!"

The two boys took off running toward the frog pond.

"Let's go along the south road and stop by Jean-Luc's house. We can see if he is finished with his dinner," suggested Gaspard.

"Good idea!"

The boys turned left and trotted onto the narrow road that led to their friend's house. Jean-Luc was the son of a well-known hunter and fur trapper. He did not live inside the town of Vincennes. His home was about a half-mile southwest of town on the banks of a small creek. It was but a short run for two energetic young boys.

As the boys got close to Jean-Luc's house they saw dust hovering above the road in the distance far to the west. The road made a wide curve in that direction as it snaked its way toward the westward settlements of Kaskaskia and Cahokia. The boys could see several men traveling on horseback, all of them headed toward Vincennes.

"There are riders coming from the west," declared Pierre. "Several of them."

"Let's go and take a look!" urged Gaspard.

The boys jumped over the ditch into the field to their right and ran through the tall grass toward the oncoming horsemen.

"Look! One of them is Father Gibault!" shouted Gaspard. The Reverend Father Francis Gibault was the parish priest who supervised the Catholic Church throughout all of the French villages in the territory. Both Pierre and Gaspard had known him all of their lives. He had baptized both boys as infants, as well as all of their siblings.

"It sure is! And the other two men in black suits are from Kaskaskia. I recognize them. I've seen both of them before when I traveled there with Papa on business," responded Pierre. "But who is that other fellow? The tall one in the buckskin clothes and the black hat is not from around here."

"I don't know, but he's huge! Look at how tall he is! At least a foot taller than Father Gibault!" exclaimed Gaspard. "And just look at the size of his horse! That is amazing! You're right. He cannot possibly be from around here!"

"No, he isn't from the Illinois Country," agreed Pierre. "He's a stranger, for sure. Let's go tell our fathers that Father Gibault is coming with some visitors!"

Gaspard slapped Pierre on the shoulder. "Race ya!"

The energetic boys took off running full-speed toward Pierre's house.

CHAPTER THREE
LISTENING THROUGH WALLS

Genevieve Grimard and Josephine Turpin both kissed their husbands and shooed them toward the street. It was time for the men to report back to the fort for militia duty. The men grabbed their hats and weapons from beneath a nearby tree and were just opening the front gate to leave when little Pierre and Gaspard suddenly came sprinting toward home along the south road. The lads were red-faced and out of breath.

"Papa! Papa!" both boys shouted. "Someone is coming!"

Gaspard chatted excitedly, "Papa, it is Father Gibault and some men from Kaskaskia. And there is a big, huge, tall, strange man with them! An enormous man! And his horse is magnificent!"

"What is the Reverend Father doing here today?" wondered Mr. Turpin aloud. "He is not due to visit and administer communion and baptisms for two more weeks."

Mr. Grimard shrugged. "I do not know. Let's go and find out."

"Can we go, too?" begged Pierre.

His father tousled the hair on his head and grinned. "Of course! Come along, boys. Let's go together and greet our visitors."

Both men and their sons ambled down Main Street toward the south, in the direction opposite the fort. Minutes later they saw the small contingent of men on horseback approaching the outskirts of town.

"The boys are right," affirmed Francois. "That's Father Gibault and some of the elders from Kaskaskia. I recognize Dr. LaFont. But who is that tall fellow in the middle?"

"I told you he was huge, Papa!" exclaimed Gaspard. "And just look at that monstrous horse!"

Mr. Grimard strained to see the strange man. Even in the saddle they could see that he was a full foot taller than the men of Kaskaskia who accompanied him. The big fellow wore clothing made of buckskin and a black hat cocked only on the left side. The hat was decorated with a fluffy black and white cockade. He carried a long rifle cradled comfortably across his lap.

"Whoever he is, he is armed extremely well. That appears to be a splendid Pennsylvania long rifle," observed Mr. Grimard. "Let's go find out what is going on."

The men and their sons walked toward the visitors. When they were about fifty yards away, the Reverend Father threw up his hand in an enthusiastic wave of recognition. They saw the Father turn and say something to his companions. Soon the group of men on horseback picked up their pace to a light trot, throwing up a dim haze of dust in their wake. They quickly reached the humble welcoming committee from Vincennes.

Mr. Grimard greeted the priest, "Hello, Father Gibault. What brings you to Vincennes at such a curious time?"

"Hello, Pierre. Hello, Francois. And hello to you, too, Gaspard and little Pierre. It is so good of you to come out and meet us. How are your families?"

Mr. Grimard responded, "They are well, Father. But tell us please, why are you here? Vincennes is in an uproar. We have heard horrible stories of atrocities to the west. Did you make your escape from the villages there?"

"Make our escape?" The priest appeared to be confused. "No, Pierre, we are here to deliver information about recent events in our towns along the Mississippi River. I brought along the elders from

Kaskaskia to share the news of the conditions in that region."

Mr. Grimard frowned. "We heard that you were invaded by some bloodthirsty Virginians. Is everyone all right in the river villages?"

Father Gibault laughed joyfully. His plump belly jiggled and his face turned bright red. "Oh, Pierre, we are just fine! Everyone is well and uninjured."

"So, the rumors are not true, then?" asked Mr. Turpin.

"Rumors?" inquired Dr. LaFont, a local physician from Kaskaskia who served as one of the village elders. "What rumors?"

"Well … there are all sorts of frightening stories circulating around Vincennes. Some say that the Virginians have killed all of the men, sold all of the women to the Indians, and roasted and eaten the children!" replied Mr. Turpin excitedly.

His enthusiastic and rather outlandish outburst elicited a loud and boisterous laugh from the strange, tall fellow in the buckskin clothes. The men from Kaskaskia joined him in good-natured laughter.

Pierre, Francois, and their two boys did not laugh. They didn't think anything that Francois Turpin said was funny.

"Those are nothing but childish rumors, Francois," declared the priest. "And they are unfounded rumors, I assure you. Roasting and eating the children! Now that's a good one! Ha!"

Mr. Turpin lowered his head in shame. "Well, Father, that's what we were told."

"You should be ashamed to believe and then share such nonsense, Francois. But enough of your silliness … we have important business at hand. Gentlemen, please allow me to make a proper introduction of our guest. Pierre Grimard and Francois Turpin, please extend a hand of fellowship to Lieutenant William Asher of the army of Virginia. He is the representative of his American commander, Colonel George Rogers Clark."

Francois Turpin and Pierre Grimard stared with open mouths and wide eyes at the strange, tall Virginian. They were dazed … confused. They offered their hands slowly and with much reservation.

The fellow spoke with a strange accent as he shook their hands. "I'm pleased to meet you fellows. Now that the introductions are over, we have much to discuss. I need you to take me to see your commander, Captain Bousseron. We must negotiate the immediate surrender of Fort Sackville."

The Virginian's face erupted into an amazingly friendly smile. Pierre Grimard and Francois Turpin simply stared at the man in wide-eyed disbelief.

Pierre and Gaspard walked to the fort with their fathers and the four visitors from the west. The lads entered the fort without anyone questioning them. Many of the little boys of Vincennes entered and exited the fort all of the time to visit with their fathers, deliver meals, or carry messages. The French officers paid them little attention. But on this day, when they arrived at Captain Bousseron's office, their fathers made little Pierre and Gaspard remain outside.

Mr. Grimard declared, "This is a military conference, boys. These men will be discussing secret matters. You cannot come inside with us."

"Oh, Papa!" wailed Pierre. "We won't get in the way. I promise."

His father placed a hand on his shoulder. "The captain would never allow it. Do as I say, Pierre. You two boys need to go back home right now. Gaspard, your father and I will be along in just a little while." He gave the boys a gentle nudge toward the front gate of the fort. "Now, get going!"

"Yes, sir," pledged Pierre.

But he and Gaspard did not leave the fort. They pretended to walk toward the gate until both of their fathers disappeared inside Captain Bousseron's office. The moment the door closed behind them little Pierre made his move.

"Come on, Gaspard! We have to find out what is happening!"

"But your papa said that we must go home," Gaspard protested.

Pierre rolled his eyes. "Just come with me!"

He grabbed Gaspard by the arm and dragged him toward the western wall of the fort. They ran beside the log walls and quickly worked their way around behind the commander's office. Once they were close to the headquarters building they hid beneath a wagon that was parked against the outer wall of the fort.

"What are we doing, Pierre?" hissed Gaspard, obviously frightened.

"We're going to listen to their parley," declared Pierre, smiling from ear to ear.

"How will we listen? And won't we get in trouble?"

Pierre pointed at the back wall of the captain's headquarters. "Look right there, beneath the window. There is a wide gap between two of the logs. We can hear everything through that hole in the wall."

"How do you know about that?" asked Gaspard, looking confused.

"Because I have listened through it before." Pierre grinned mischievously. "I spy on things around here all of the time, especially since the British left."

"Why, Pierre?"

"Because it's fun, Gaspard! Besides, it's only the militia. We don't have to be afraid of the French soldiers … not like we feared the British. These men are our neighbors and friends."

"I suppose you're right," admitted Gaspard. He grinned. "It does sound like an adventure. So, what do we do now?"

"Just follow me!"

Pierre scurried toward the wall and leaned in close to the hole between the logs. Gaspard followed him. Pierre lifted his finger to his lips, urging Gaspard to remain silent. Then both boys placed their ears to the wide crack in the walls. They heard the distinctive voice of Captain Bousseron as he conducted the meeting inside his office. They also heard whispers and mumbling among the other officers and men.

Bousseron almost shouted, "And you are certain of this information, Father Gibault? You have verified the sources?"

"Yes, Francois. As I have already told you, Colonel Clark presented documents and newspapers from the east to verify his claims. The Kingdom of France declared war against Great Britain on March 17 of this year. Our mother country is, most definitely, at war with England."

Pierre slapped Gaspard on the arm and whispered, "France has entered the war!"

"What war?"

"The American Revolution!"

"What does that mean to us?" hissed Gaspard.

"I don't know yet. Just keep listening …"

Captain Bousseron asked another question. "Have the Americans treated you well?"

Father Gibault responded, "Oh, quite well, Francois. At first, we assumed that we would have our lands and property taken from us and that the men would all be carried off to a military prison. But Colonel Clark has been most kind and generous. He has allowed us to choose our own side in their revolutionary conflict. He freely offered an oath of allegiance to Virginia and the United States. Most of our citizens have already pledged their oath."

"And you wish for us to take this oath?" asked the captain.

Father Gibault responded, "That is why we have come today. Rather than appearing with a large army, Colonel Clark thought it best to send one of his officers and a group of local leaders from Kaskaskia to talk to the leaders and citizens of Vincennes."

There was a brief silence, then Captain Bousseron asked, "And if we take this oath to Virginia, what then? What will become of our village? What will happen to the fort and our own militia?"

The boys then heard the strange voice of the American officer. "Your militia will remain as they are and you will continue as their commander, Captain. Colonel Clark will assign an officer of the rank of captain or higher to assume command of the fort, itself. But you will remain as the head of the local militia. Indeed, we will rely upon your men for the proper defense of this fort and village."

"Are you saying that if we swear your oath we will become soldiers for the American cause?" Captain Bousseron asked bluntly.

The American responded, "Yes, sir. That is exactly what I am saying. If your men swear their allegiance to Virginia and the Congress of the United States, your people will become citizens of the United States of America. I will, this very day, record your enlistments in our army and place your names on the muster roll and payroll."

There was a time of awkward silence. The boys heard a boot scuff the floor. They heard someone cough. They could even hear a lot of heavy, excited breathing, but no one was talking.

Finally, Father Gibault spoke again. "Surely you see the wisdom in pursuing this wise path, Francois. These Long Knives from Virginia are very powerful. Their war against England is gaining strength. France has chosen the side of the United States and is now at war with England!"

Father Gibault paused to allow his words to sink in. "These mighty armies are about to clash right here on our very own soil, among our fields and homes. The Virginians have been good to our people and made clear their desire for our freedom and prosperity. They treat us as equals, not as subjects. I urge you to follow the lead of the other villages and take their oath."

There was another long, silent pause. Gaspard and Pierre were breathless as they strained to hear the outcome of the meeting.

Once again, Father Gibault broke the uncomfortable silence. "Francois … Captain Bousseron. What are you thinking? What do you intend to do?"

The captain responded, "Gentlemen, this is not a decision that I can make for an entire village. I know what I plan to do. But each man and each family must make their own decision. I will not force a single citizen of Vincennes to conform to my politics, or to yours, Father." He paused. "We must allow the people to decide for themselves."

The captain then spoke with authority to his other officers. "Men, sound the alarm and notify the citizens that there will be a town meeting in one hour. All men age sixteen and older are expected to be present. This meeting will take place at the church, if that is agreeable with you, Father Gibault."

The priest responded, "Most agreeable, Francois, and an excellent idea."

"Very well then. Off you go, men. Inform the people. In one hour's time we will meet and choose sides in this war of rebellion against England."

There were loud noises from inside the office as chairs began to move and men rose to their feet.

They heard the door open on the far side of the room and the men chatting excitedly as they departed the office and walked into the courtyard of the fort. The room on the other side of the log wall quickly fell silent.

Gaspard stared wide-eyed at Pierre. "What does that all mean? What were they talking about, Pierre?"

"It means that we might be going to war against England!"

Gaspard's eyes opened even wider.

Suddenly a stern voice yelled from the direction of the water well in the nearby corner of the fort. The man exclaimed, "Hey! What are you kids doing over there?" A militia soldier began to walk quickly in their direction.

Pierre slapped Gaspard on the leg. "Let's get out of here!"

The boys jumped to their feet and took off running in the opposite direction.

CHAPTER FOUR
A SPY IN THE CHURCH

Pierre was frustrated. He simply could not get his friends to agree to a plan to sneak into the church and spy on the upcoming meeting of the men of the village. The five boys … Pierre, Gaspard, Jean-Luc, Adrien, and Quentin … were gathered for a "secret" meeting of their aspiring spy network at Pierre Grimard's grain mill. Little Pierre knew that his father's place of business was closed for the day because of the militia muster. It was well away from the fort and the church. That made it the perfect place for a meeting of the band of young spies.

The boys sat cross-legged in a dark corner of the stone building. No one seemed to be paying much attention to Pierre's arguments and pleading.

"We have to get inside that church!" hissed Pierre. "We just have to!"

"But how?" asked Adrien. "That tiny building will be packed with people. Didn't you say that every man over age sixteen will be there?"

Pierre nodded sadly.

"Then surely there will be no room!" declared Quentin. "And we certainly cannot dig a tunnel under the floor. It could cave in and cause the whole church to collapse." He giggled teasingly and punched Gaspard in the shoulder.

"Ha, ha, ha. Very funny," retorted Gaspard, obviously not amused.

Jean-Luc ignored their banter. "There are definitely not enough seats. Men will be sitting in the floor and standing along the walls. Some may even have to stand outside and listen through the windows."

Gaspard exclaimed, "I told you, Pierre! We won't be able to go in there during their big parley. Even if there was some room, they likely wouldn't allow us inside the church, anyway. This is grown-up stuff, and it sounds really serious. They're talking about taking oaths and making war."

"I suppose you're right," admitted Pierre. "But I so wanted to hear what the men had to say. I wanted us to be the first ones in town to hear their decision! That's what real spies do, fellows. They discover secrets."

"We'll find out soon enough," responded Adrien. "I'm sure that the word will get out pretty quickly. You know how the news travels fast in this little village." He grinned. "The moment that the meeting is over all Captain Bousseron has to do is go and tell Mrs. Descoteaux what occurred. That old bat will tell everyone within fifty miles before supper time!"

The boys rolled with laughter. They knew all too well how the nosy old woman liked to share juicy news and gossip, especially when she was sworn to secrecy!

"The only problem with that strategy is that she will add to the story and make some stuff up," declared Quentin. "By the time the news gets to the outskirts of Vincennes people will think we are at war with the Spaniards in St. Louis!"

Again, the boys laughed uproariously. It was, indeed, true. Mrs. Descoteaux, the well-known town gossip, was prone to exaggeration and intentionally sharing false and misleading information.

"It is settled, then," declared Quentin. "We go home and wait for our fathers to tell us the news."

The boys stared at one another in dejected silence.

Pierre sighed in disappointment. "I suppose."

"Good." Jean-Luc stood quickly and stretched. "It is almost time for my afternoon snack and nap." He grinned and cut his eyes at the other boys. "Mrs. Duvalier has two pies cooling in her window. One of them is cherry. I saw the red juice that bubbled through the crust and dried on top. How about we go on a different spy mission and see if we can capture a pie and then sneak off to the pond?"

"Yes! And we can hide the evidence in our bellies!" proclaimed Gaspard.

"I'm in!" declared Quentin.

"I'm in," echoed Adrien.

The four boys stared at Pierre and waited for his answer.

Pierre shook his head. "I can't, guys. I really need to get home and check on Mama and my brothers. I'm sure that she has some chores for me."

"Well, I would say that we will save you a piece of pie …" began Jean-Luc.

Quentin finished his sentence, "… but we can't leave any evidence lying around."

"Thanks, anyway, guys. You go have some fun. I will be back here at the mill after supper, just before sunset. Come back if you can and we will make plans for tomorrow. Agreed?"

"Agreed!" responded the four boys.

All five of the lads darted out of the open door of the mill. The four pie-stealers scurried along toward Mrs. Duvalier's house on the south side of the village. Pierre went in the other direction, toward his house. But he was not going to his house. He had another plan and another destination in mind.

Instead, Pierre ran alone toward the little church next to Fort Sackville.

Pierre gasped for a breath of fresh air. It was so unbelievably hot. He lay hidden in the only secret place that he could think of within the church. He sat on the uncomfortable stool inside the priest's tiny confessional chamber. Once inside he had pulled the wool curtain closed across the door. There was no ventilation inside the small wooden booth. Little Pierre was drowning in sweat. He thought he might suffocate. He felt as though he might pass out. He fanned his face with his hand, but it didn't seem to help at all.

It was bad enough that it was the month of July and the middle of the afternoon, which was always the hottest part of the day. When you combined the stifling, humid heat of summer with a room full of warm, sweaty, stinky humans conditions became almost unbearable.

Pierre wasn't alone in his suffering. The air throughout the tiny church was stifling, and it seemed that the tempers of some of the men of Vincennes were beginning to burn along with the oppressive summer heat. Their discussion was animated and sometimes angry. The men of the village seemed to be indecisive and frustrated. Some men stomped their feet. They wanted to swear the oath. Others pleaded for wisdom and moderation, and discouraged anyone from signing the oath. Still more shouted with fervor and emotion.

Finally, the shrill voice of Father Gibault caused the noisy room to become silent and reverent. "Friends! Stop! We have been at this for an hour or more, and we are beginning to endure the same questions already asked and answered. No more pointless talking! The time has come for your decision!"

Pierre grinned. He liked Father Gibault. The man had spunk. The gathering seemed to grow calmer after the Reverend Father spoke.

The priest continued, "Men of Vincennes, I submit to you that there is no need to resist this army from Virginia. I urge you, as souls under my charge, to follow both my counsel and my example and swear this oath. I implore you to unite yourselves with the United States of America and the causes of freedom and liberty for which the people of this brand-new nation are now fighting. If you are willing, I am prepared to administer the oath given me by Colonel Clark. Right here. Right now."

There was more groaning, mumbling, and chatter. Clearly, the men did not know what to do. Even from deep inside his hiding spot in the priest's confession chamber, Pierre could hear the fear in the voices of the men. Suddenly, the lad's heart jumped into his throat when he heard his father's voice rise above the other voices in the crowd.

"Father Gibault, if I may … I would like to ask one final question before I am prepared to render my own decision."

"Yes, Pierre. What is your question?" The chubby priest sounded frustrated.

"I need to know the intent of Captain Bousseron. What is he planning to do?"

"That is an excellent question, Pierre," affirmed Father Gibault.

There was a pause, and then little Pierre heard the priest declare, "Francois, one of your men has an important question for you."

Then little Pierre heard his father speak again. "Francois, what would you have us do, old friend? What are you planning to do?"

Again, there was a long, dramatic pause. Little Pierre strained to hear the captain's response. He jumped in surprise when the captain's voice boomed from a spot very near the confessional. The man was, apparently, sitting right beside the booth where Pierre had hidden!

The captain declared, "Pierre, the decision is surprisingly simple for me. The allegiance of my heart is to Vincennes. The allegiance of my blood is to France. I have absolutely no love for the British. I have no allegiance, at all, to King George or Great

Britain. I serve them now only because of a treaty signed many years ago and thousands of miles away from here by men I do not know. But here, today, I get to make my own choice."

He continued, "I believe, based upon their actions here in Illinois, that the intent of the Americans is liberty and freedom from tyranny. Therefore, I plan to join with their cause. I will swear their oath and join their army."

A rumble of excitement erupted throughout the room. Little Pierre smiled silently and proudly. He felt a great admiration for Mr. Bousseron. But his pride truly swelled when he heard his father's voice once again.

"Captain, if you will swear the oath and join the Americans today, then so will I!"

Another voice thundered, "As will I!"

That was the voice of Francois Turpin, Gaspard's father! Little Pierre could barely control his excitement. Immediately, one after another and in rapid succession, every man of Vincennes stood and proclaimed his intent to join the Americans. Boots and moccasins scooted loudly across the rough boards of the floor. It sounded like one of the pew benches in the church actually turned over. The moment was electrifying. The room seemed filled with passion, excitement, and boldness. The men cheered and clapped.

The voice of Father Gibault rose over the loud celebration and called out, "Lieutenant Asher, you have heard the declarations of the men of Vincennes. Do I have your permission to administer the oath?"

The unusual voice of the American officer responded, "You do indeed, Reverend Father! And once sworn, I ask that each man come forward and add his name to my list. It will be the muster roll and pay sheet that I will forward to Colonel Clark."

Father Gibault declared, "Very well, then. Men of Vincennes, please raise your right hands."

Pierre could hear the pride in the priest's voice, but he paid absolutely no attention to the words of the oath or the other speeches spoken by the men inside the church. He was too excited, and he was so very proud of his brave father who had spoken out boldly in the middle of all the arguments and confusion.

Minutes later the meeting was adjourned. Pierre listened silently and gasped for fresh air as he waited for the room to empty. The men signed the roll sheet as rapidly as possible and sprinted for the door, each one in search of fresh air and a drink of cool water. Soon the building was silent and empty. Pierre reached up to pull back the curtain and make his exit, but he froze in horror when he heard the familiar voice of Father Gibault.

"You can come out now, Pierre. I know you're in there."

Pierre sighed reluctantly and pulled the curtain to one side. The dark brown robe of the priest was the first thing he saw. The clergyman stood just outside the booth with both hands resting on his wide hips. A huge smile filled his face.

"What's the matter, Pierre? Did you actually think I did not know that someone was hiding inside my own confessional booth?"

Pierre grinned mischievously. "I just wanted to be the first one to hear the decision, Father." He decided to try and change the subject. "Aren't you proud of my papa? I know I am!"

Father Gibault threw back his head and laughed. "Get out of here, you little spy! And no more snooping inside my church!"

He gave Pierre a swat on the backside as the boy darted past him and ran toward the door.

CHAPTER FIVE
AN ALMOST AMERICAN FLAG

Vincennes - August 25, 1778

"What is your report, gentlemen?" Pierre demanded with an air of authority. He gazed at the blank, listless stares of his pals Jean-Luc, Adrien, and Quentin.

Pierre was busy conducting the latest meeting of the secret band of adventurous little spies of Vincennes. The boys were hiding in their old shack beside the river. The mouth of their collapsed tunnel was now covered with a large board. Jean-Luc had painted the words "KEEP OUT" in bold letters on the board back at the beginning of the summer. The boys never again ventured into that dark, dangerous hole in the ground.

Pierre was asking for a report from the group because the other boys had recently elected Pierre as their "captain of spies." The mission of their secret organization was to keep watch on all military and war matters within Fort Sackville and the village of Vincennes. As their commander, Pierre led all of their meetings and made duty assignments for the other four boys.

Thus far their spy business had not been much of an adventure, at all. The boys infiltrated the fort on a regular basis and kept watch along the roads, but nothing exciting ever happened. There were no British soldiers to fight, no shooting, and no battles. Even the Indians seemed more peaceful and rarely caused trouble in the town. There was, basically, no excitement at all to be found in or near the village.

The simple truth was that nothing had really changed in Vincennes after that dramatic day when the men swore their oaths to Virginia and the United States. The tall American departed on his monstrous horse three days later and had not returned. The Frenchmen of Vincennes continued with their regular jobs and performed occasional militia duties at the fort. But that was it. There was nothing else going on. It was, in a word, boring.

"Where is Gaspard, anyway?" demanded Pierre. "He's never been late for one of our meetings."

The other three boys looked at one another and shrugged.

"You fellows sure don't know much. You can't even keep up with one of our own gang. I guess that makes you a pretty rotten bunch of spies!" declared Pierre.

"Well you don't know where he is, either!" retorted Quentin. "He's your best friend, after all. It seems to me that the 'king of the spies' would know where his best buddy is."

The other boys snickered. Pierre was just opening his mouth to respond when Gaspard came bursting through the fragile door of the dilapidated shack. His face was blood-red, sweat poured from his brow, and he could barely breathe.

"What is wrong, Gaspard?" demanded Pierre. "Were you being chased?" He darted toward the door and glanced outside to ensure that Gaspard had not been followed.

Gaspard shook his head and attempted to catch his breath. He managed to get out two desperate words: "He's … back …"

"Who is back, Gaspard? Who are you talking about?" demanded Pierre.

Gaspard sucked in a huge breath. "The big … American. Lieutenant … Asher …."

"The American has returned?" shouted Quentin gleefully.

Gaspard nodded. "And two others … are with him." His breathing was beginning to slow.

"Two more Americans?" asked Jean-Luc excitedly.

Gaspard simply nodded. "I need to sit down."

"Yes, Gaspard, sit down and rest. Adrien, get him some water!" ordered Pierre.

The boy fetched a gourd full of water and brought it to Gaspard, who took a long, deep drink.

Pierre gave the boy a moment to compose himself, then asked, "Where did you see them, Gaspard?"

"On the road from Kaskaskia. They were almost to Vincennes. They should be arriving at the fort at any moment now."

Pierre's eyes lit up. "All right, fellows. It's time to get to work! We have to find out what the Americans are doing and why they are here. Gaspard, you stay here and rest a while longer. We will return soon. You can keep an eye on our headquarters. Adrien, you will go with me. We will sneak inside the fort and work our way behind Captain Bousseron's headquarters so that we can listen through the wall. Jean-Luc and Quentin, we need you to get the attention of the guards at the gate so that we can sneak inside."

"How in the world will we do that?" asked Quentin.

Jean-Luc patted his partner reassuringly on the shoulder. "Don't worry about it, Quentin. We can do this. Trust me."

Pierre asked, "Is everyone ready?"

The boys nodded and smiled.

"Good! Then let's go. We meet back here in one hour!"

The Americans had already entered Fort Sackville when the boys made their move at the gate. Pierre and Adrien snuck close to the gate on the east side and hid behind a large pile of logs. They could see the Americans inside the fort as they tied the reins of their horses to a small bush. They could also see Quentin and Jean-Luc walking from one of the stores on Main Street and heading directly toward the gate. The boys simply ambled along like they were out for an ordinary, everyday Sunday walk.

Suddenly one of the guards challenged the boys. "Where do you two lads think you're going?"

"To the fort, of course," answered Jean-Luc. "We have business inside."

The fellow chuckled and looked sarcastically at his friend. "Oh, so you have business, huh? What kind of business would that be?"

Jean-Luc walked up directly in front of the man and growled, "None of your business!"

He then kicked the man soundly in the shin with his right foot. The sound of his leather shoe made a loud and distinctive "pop" against the man's skin bone. The fellow squealed in pain.

He screamed, "I'm going to get you, you little scoundrel!"

He lunged at Jean-Luc and tried to grab his arm. The boy jerked away and yelled at Quentin, "Run!"

The two mischievous boys took off running toward the center of the village.

The wounded guard shrieked, "Let's catch those rascals, Lamont!"

Both men took off running after Quentin and Jean-Luc, abandoning their guard post, and leaving the gate unattended. Pierre and Adrien stepped from behind the pile of logs and ambled nonchalantly through the gate. Once inside the walls they took off running along the familiar route that led them to their secret place behind Captain Bousseron's office. In less than a minute they were kneeling at the back wall and listening to the men conversing inside the military headquarters.

The boys heard the familiar voice of Captain Bousseron. "Captain Helm, gentlemen of Virginia, I welcome you to Fort Sackville."

"Ahh … that is incorrect, sir," an unfamiliar voice responded.

"Pardon me?" inquired Bousseron.

"Colonel Clark has discarded that name. He considered it inappropriate for us to continue using a title of British choosing. He has officially renamed this post with the name Fort Patrick Henry, in honor of the great governor of Virginia."

"Very well, then, Captain Helm. Fort Patrick Henry it is. I assume that you will want to take ownership of this workspace. I will, of course, vacate my office and surrender it to you as the new commandant of this fort."

"Oh, no, Captain Bousseron! I would not dream of displacing you from your headquarters. I am quite sure that we can make other arrangements within the fort. I would like to have a space that could be utilized both for my command office as well as my own personal quarters. Is there such a space available?"

Captain Bousseron responded, "Certainly, sir. The ground floor blockhouse on the northeast corner is spacious and well-suited for your purposes. We have a few items stored in there, but I can have my men remove them to another location immediately. Now, will you be needing anything else?"

The newcomer responded, "Yes, Captain. We require a flag for the fort."

"A flag?" inquired Captain Bousseron.

"Yes, Captain! A flag! That's what this post needs! A unique flag that demonstrates the fort and village's allegiance to Virginia and the United States."

"But we do not have an American flag," explained the captain. "Frankly, we do not even know what one looks like."

"It has thirteen stripes to represent the thirteen states," answered the man called Captain Helm.

"That does not help much," retorted Bousseron. "Besides, colored cloth is very rare here, indeed. And that is what you would need for a flag. We may not be able to find cloth in the colors that you require."

Captain Helm responded, "We would need red, white, and blue. Those are the colors of our nation's flag."

Bousseron shook his head. "Impossible. There is no blue to be found here. I can promise you that right now. I have never seen it used in Vincennes. Likely there is no white, either."

"Well then, what colors do you think may be available?"

"Mrs. St. Marie recently completed a project for me using red cloth. That is most likely the color of cloth that will be readily available here in Vincennes. After that, your guess is as good as mine. We may be able to find you some green."

"Green?" the man thundered. "There is no green in the American flag!"

"Maybe so, but those are the two colors that you are likely to find around here. They actually represent our area very well. Local Indian tribes trade in beads that are red and green. They have long represented the colors of the Wabash River."

"Is that so?" pondered Helm. "Then that just may be the perfect answer. A simple flag of thirteen stripes of alternating red and green. It will be the Fort Patrick Henry flag!"

"Are you willing to spend significant money for such a flag? The cloth will be expensive, as well as the seamstress costs."

"Of course, of course," responded Captain Helm. "Whatever it takes. I will issue a certificate of reimbursement, payable by the state of Virginia."

"Very well, Captain Helm. I will see that it gets done."

"Excellent, Captain Bousseron! Please work quickly. I want to see that flag flying proudly over this American fort by the end of the next week."

"Of course, Captain Helm. I will contact the ladies immediately."

The boys listened to the sounds of shuffling feet inside the office, then the creaking of the door. The three Americans and Captain Bousseron departed quickly.

Adrien looked confused. "What was that all about?" he hissed at Pierre.

"The Americans have taken command of the fort, and they want an American flag to fly on the pole."

"But that strange man said that the American flag is red, white, and blue. I have never, ever seen any blue cloth in Vincennes. Have you?"

Pierre shrugged. "Well, then ... I guess that it will be an almost American flag." He grinned. "Let's go tell the others what has happened!"

The boys easily snuck through the gate of the newly renamed Fort Patrick Henry. They made their way back to the secret shack and made their report to the other boys in their secret spy ring. Jean-Luc and Quentin recounted the hilarious story of the two guards, one of them limping horribly from Jean-Luc's vicious kick to the shin, who chased them for almost a half-hour throughout the streets and alleys of Vincennes. The boys laughed so hard that their sides ached.

The young spies stayed in their hideout until it was almost dark and then returned to their homes to complete their chores and eat hot, delicious suppers. They slept soundly that night and dreamed about more courageous spying adventures.

The following day Captain Bousseron hired Madame Marie Goderre as seamstress for the Fort Patrick Henry flag. He paid her a very good salary in gold coin. She managed to locate plenty of red and green cloth. She also recruited three other women to help in the project. They completed their work in a remarkably short period of time.

Less than a week later the large, beautiful flag of seven red and six green stripes flew high atop the pole of Fort Patrick Henry. The massive banner measured almost seven feet across. There was even enough cloth left over for a smaller flag, which Captain Helm placed on a pole beside the small dock on the bank of the Wabash River.

There could be no doubt about it now. Vincennes was an American town. Fort Patrick Henry was an American military outpost. And America was at war with Great Britain.

But, as usual, the people of Vincennes went about their normal, everyday business. Most of them assumed that the war would never touch their quiet, peaceful town on the frontier. They doubted that they would ever see another British soldier.

But they were wrong … very, very wrong.

Part II

The Redcoats Return

CHAPTER SIX
THE MISSING PATROL

December 1, 1778

Little Pierre sat on the foot of the bed and watched as his father packed his haversack full of food and supplies. He was very sad. His father was leaving on a militia patrol.

"How long will you be gone, Papa?"

"I do not know, Pierre. This is a long-range patrol to the north along the Wabash River. At least a week, maybe more."

The boy pleaded, "But why do you have to go?"

His father stopped putting his belongings into the bag and placed his hand gently on his son's shoulder. "Because I am a sergeant now. I have responsibilities. I am in command of the men on this patrol." He resumed his work of packing. "We must be on constant lookout for the British."

Little Pierre's eyes lit up with excitement. "The British soldiers are returning to Vincennes?"

"We do not know for sure, son, but there are rumors. Some of the Indian tribes to the north have reported a large force of Redcoats headed this way. That is why Captain Bousseron is sending us in that direction on patrol."

"I want to go, Papa!"

Pierre Grimard smiled. "No, son. You must stay here and be in charge of the house. You are nine years old now. I am counting on you to take care of your mother and brothers for me."

Little Pierre nodded and rolled his eyes ever so slightly. Fathers always said stuff like that to their sons when they were going away on long trips. But little boys knew full well that their mothers were the ones who were really in charge of things around the house, whether their fathers were home or not.

"How will you travel? Will you walk?" little Pierre inquired.

"No, son. The forest is too thick and there has been too much rain. We will take two canoes several miles upriver. Francois Turpin will go with me, along with three other men. We will pick a good place to make camp on high ground and then keep watch over the river."

"Is that how the British will come? On the Wabash?"

His father nodded. “Of course. It is the only ‘road’ to Vincennes from the north, and the only way to move an army. So we will keep a sharp eye on the river. If we catch sight of them we will paddle our canoes quickly downstream to warn the captain and the other soldiers at the fort.”

Pierre listened thoughtfully. He didn’t like the idea of the British returning, but it would certainly be more exciting than the painfully dull boredom of the past several months.

“Do you really think they will come back, Papa?”

His father smiled grimly. “I hope not, son. I truly hope not.”

“It’s cold in here, Pierre!” complained Adrien. “Hurry up! I want to go home!”

The five young spies of Vincennes were huddled together in a small circle inside their secret shack. They had just arrived for a quick conference to share news about events around the village. The unusually bitter December cold made their meeting place almost unbearable. They dared not build a fire for fear of revealing their secret location. This was, most likely, going to be a very short spy meeting.

"Has anyone heard any fresh news?" asked Pierre.

"There are rumors everywhere," answered Quentin, rubbing his hands together in an effort to keep them warm. "The entire town seems to have gone crazy. Everyone says that the British are coming back. They're frightened."

Jean-Luc nodded. "My Papa has started hiding our things."

"What do you mean?" asked Pierre.

"He's hiding the furs he has harvested, our food supplies, and all of our lead and gunpowder. He has most of it stashed in a cave that only he knows about, but he buried the powder and lead. He says that's the first stuff that the Redcoats will try to take when they come back."

"If they come back," Pierre corrected him.

"Oh, they're coming back. My papa says so," declared Adrien. "Some are so convinced of the British coming back that they are leaving Vincennes."

"Leaving?" exclaimed Pierre. "I have not heard about this!"

Adrien nodded. "My papa has sold two canoes and built four other small boats for people headed downriver to flee the British."

"Where will they go?" asked Quentin.

Adrien shrugged. "I don't know. Just away from here."

"It does sound like the entire village is in an uproar," declared Pierre. "We must increase our spy missions. We have to find out about the British! We need more information!"

Gaspard hadn't spoken a single word since he arrived. He looked very sad and upset. His eyes were swollen a bit and looked as if he had been crying.

Pierre asked, "What's the matter with you, Gaspard?"

The glum boy didn't make eye contact with the others. He just kept staring at the bare ground in the center of their circle.

"Gaspard?" Pierre inquired again.

The forlorn boy raised his head slowly and looked at his pals. "Things are bad at home. My mama is so sad all of the time. She cries day and night." His lip quivered just a bit. "I don't like to see her this way."

"Why is she so upset?" asked Jean-Luc.

"Because Papa has been gone for so long. He and Mr. Grimard and the other men on the patrol have been gone for almost two weeks, and we haven't heard a single word from them for many days now." He paused thoughtfully. "Mama is convinced that something terrible has happened to them. That must be why the messages from them have stopped." He looked sadly at Pierre. "Your mother is going to visit Captain Bousseron this afternoon to demand information about our fathers."

Pierre was surprised, and a little bit upset, that his mother had not told him about this upcoming meeting with the captain of the militia. He smiled and attempted to reassure his friend.

"Do not worry, Gaspard. I will find out what is going on. Your father and my father are just fine. You'll see."

Gaspard wiped his nose and smiled. "I hope they're all right. I miss my papa. He's never been gone from home this long."

"I miss my papa, too. But it's during times like these that we have to stick together. Right, guys?"

The other boys answered in unison, "Right!"

It took quite a bit of begging, but Pierre somehow managed to convince his mother to allow him to attend her meeting with Captain Bousseron. She made Pierre promise that he would sit quietly and not say a word. He agreed. They left his younger brothers with Mrs. Turpin and made the short walk to Fort Patrick Henry.

The captain welcomed them warmly and invited them to sit in comfortable chairs beside his toasty fireplace. The militia commander wasted no time getting to the subject of the visit.

"I understand that you are upset with our current situation. What, exactly, are your concerns, Genevieve?" inquired Captain Bousseron.

"My concerns, Francois? Well, my one and only concern is the fact that my husband is missing! I have not heard a single word from him in over a week! Shouldn't he have returned to the fort by now?"

"Genevieve, you know that Pierre and his men are on a long-range patrol, very far to the north. It should come as no surprise that they have not yet returned."

"But shouldn't we have received some word? A note from a messenger? Something?" She was almost hysterical.

He agreed, "It is a bit odd that we have received no reports from him in the past five days. But there could be any number of explanations for that. He may have moved his team upriver for a better vantage point. There were heavy rains a few days ago. They may be dealing with swollen creeks and streams. My dear, it is best not to jump to any wild conclusions. You must be patient and have faith."

He stood and walked around the desk, extending his hand to Genevieve in a most gentlemanly manner. She took his hand and rose to her feet. Little Pierre stood, as well. The captain escorted both of them toward the door.

"Mrs. Grimard, I urge you to return to your home, care for your children, and wait patiently. You must assume the best, not the worst. The moment that I receive word from your husband, I will send a runner to fetch you. All right?" He smiled warmly.

"Yes, Francois. You're right, of course. I need to remain calm. I need to have faith in my husband." She smiled at the captain. "I am grateful for your time."

"You are most welcome, Genevieve. My door is always open to you and to any of the other wives of my men."

Captain Bousseron was just about to reach for the latch on the door when the heavy wooden portal suddenly exploded open in his face. He had to block the door with his foot to keep it from slamming into Mrs. Grimard.

He scolded the young private who had burst into his office. "Philippe, what is your reason for barging into my office in such a rush? You almost injured Mrs. Grimard!"

"I'm sorry, sir. But a runner just returned from upriver! The British are upon us! They are camped only two miles to our north! Surely they will invade tomorrow!"

"Good God!" exclaimed the captain.

"That's not all, sir." The soldier reached into his shooting pouch and pulled out a crumpled, folded paper marked with a red wax seal. "The runner brought this letter, given to him under parley, by a British officer in one of their forward patrols. Our runner was instructed to deliver it only to you, Captain, and not to the commander of the Virginians."

Captain Bousseron reached for the note with a trembling hand. He carefully broke the wax seal and unfolded the letter. He scanned its words quickly. His face became gray and pale.

"What does it say, Francois?" demanded Genevieve Grimard.

The captain cleared his throat and read the note aloud.

To the Commander of the French Militia in Vincennes,

The combined armies of Great Britain and her Indian allies are within striking distance of your village. We will enter your town and lay siege upon Fort Sackville before noon tomorrow. The French militiamen in the fort are hereby ordered to lay down their weapons and return to their homes in peace.

If you do not resist, you will be treated fairly and allowed to pursue your daily lifestyles, work, and businesses. There will be no harsh consequences for your recent mutinous alliance with the Virginia rebels. You will be given new oaths to King George III and welcomed gladly back into protection of the British Empire.

However, if you do not lay down your weapons immediately, I will regard the entire village as being hostile to the British Crown. I will unleash the several hundred Indians under my command to enter and utterly destroy your town.

Signed,
Henry Hamilton, Lieutenant Governor - Fort Detroit

Pierre could not believe what he had just heard! The Redcoats were on the verge of invading

Vincennes! They had Indians with them, ready to attack the village!

He stared in disbelief at his mother. She looked strange. Something was wrong with her.

"Mama, are you all right?"

Genevieve Grimard looked sadly at her son, made brief eye contact with Captain Bousseron, and then her eyes rolled back in her head as she collapsed and fainted.

CHAPTER SEVEN
PREPARING FOR THE ENEMY

Pierre did not know what to do to help his mother. He was just glad that Captain Bousseron had been there to catch her when she fell.

The captain nodded toward his large desk chair. "Pierre, pull the chair out from behind my desk and place it in the corner."

"Yes, sir." Pierre obeyed immediately.

Captain Bousseron carried Genevieve Grimard toward the large, comfortable chair. He carefully laid her down on the padded seat and rested her head against the corner. Her face was as pale as a clean, white sheet. Pierre was terribly worried.

Captain Bousseron turned to the man who had delivered the British message to his office. "Philippe,

I want you to go and find Lieutenant Armand and bring him here immediately. And spread the word among the other officers to report to me as quickly as possible."

The man saluted and answered, "Right away, sir!" He turned and ran quickly out of Bousseron's office.

"Pierre, bring me that pitcher of water and the washcloth. We need to revive your mother."

Pierre fetched the pitcher of water and cloth from the wash table and carried it to the captain. The militia officer doused the cloth with the cold water and placed it in Pierre's hand. "Wipe your mother's face with this. Speak gently to her. She should awaken in a short while. Do not worry, Pierre. She is just fine. Women sometimes do this when they are upset … or when they are expecting a child." He smiled at Pierre.

Captain Bousseron marched over to the door and called for some militiamen who were standing outside in the courtyard of the fort. Three soldiers instantly answered his call.

The captain pointed at Pierre's mother. "Gentlemen, I need you to help Mrs. Grimard back to her home. Once she is safely there, I want you to go and fetch Mrs. Turpin to stay with her. When you are certain of her safety you must return to the fort immediately. The French militia will meet within the hour. Do you understand?"

All three men responded, "Yes, sir." They placed their weapons against the wall and began to tend to Genevieve. Her eyes fluttered slightly as she began to awaken.

"Come with me, Pierre." The captain walked out of the door onto the porch. Pierre tossed the cloth into the water basin and followed him. Once outside Captain Bousseron knelt down and placed his hand on Pierre's shoulder. "Son, I probably should not have read the note in your presence. I need you to keep secret everything that you heard here this afternoon. Do you understand?"

Pierre nodded. "I understand, Captain. What are you going to do? What will you tell the American officer?"

Captain Bousseron grinned proudly at Pierre. "You are a smart little lad, aren't you?"

"Smart enough to know that you have a decision to make … whether the men of Vincennes will surrender or stand with the Americans and fight the British and their Indians."

The captain nodded grimly. "It is a difficult decision for me, Pierre."

"I know that you will do what is right for Vincennes, Captain."

Pierre's mother appeared at the door. She was still shaky, but able to walk. A militiaman stood on each side of her, supporting her arms to help her stand.

One stood behind her just in case she happened to faint again. She seemed a bit embarrassed.

She declared, "Captain Bousseron, I sincerely apologize for my female silliness. I do not know what came over me."

"The news shocked you, Mrs. Grimard. There is nothing for which you need to feel ashamed. The promise that I made to you earlier still remains. The moment that I hear something about your husband I will send for you."

She nodded. "Come, Pierre. Let us return home."

Captain Bousseron interjected, "Would it be possible for me to borrow your son for the remainder of the day, Mrs. Grimard? I find myself short of runners, and he would be most useful to me here at the fort this afternoon."

Pierre's mother eyed both the captain and Pierre suspiciously. It appeared that she might deny the request. Pierre was beyond thrilled when she answered, "I suppose that would be all right. But I would want him home in time for supper."

"Suppertime might be difficult. I will see that the boy is fed here at the fort. How about bedtime tonight?" He paused. "I could really use the extra help, Genevieve."

She reluctantly nodded her assent.

"Bedtime it is, then," responded the captain. "Meanwhile, my men will see you home and safely in the care of Mrs. Turpin."

"Thank you, Francois." She turned and walked with the three officers toward the gate of the fort.

The captain waited until she was out of earshot, then whispered to Pierre, "I know that you have been snooping around outside my office, Pierre. You have been listening to our private conversations."

Pierre stared at the captain wide-eyed. He didn't say a word. Fear gripped his heart. What would the captain do? Pierre thought, "Is he going to punish me?"

"You have turned into quite an industrious little spy, haven't you?"

Again, Pierre just stared. He simply did not know what to say.

Captain Bousseron sighed deeply. "I suppose that if you plan to be a spy in my fort, it would be best if you were actually working for me. Does that sound agreeable to you?"

Pierre grinned and nodded.

"All right then, Pierre. I have a mission for you. Are you up to it?"

Pierre nodded excitedly. "Absolutely, sir! Just tell me what you need me to do."

"I want you to find the American, Captain Helm, and keep an eye on him for me. See if he acts in any way like he knows about the British coming. He is probably just lounging around his quarters, as usual. Don't talk to him. Just watch him. Report back to me just before sunset. I will meet with our militia before that time. Then I will send you to fetch him to my office so I can tell him what the French militiamen are planning to do. Can you handle that important assignment?"

"You can count on me, sir!"

Captain Bousseron chuckled. "I knew that I could."

The sun had just gone down. The Frenchmen had made their decision. They were not going to resist the British. The men were in agreement that they could not take any action that might endanger their homes and families. Governor Hamilton's threat to unleash his Indian horde upon the village was enough to make the Frenchmen lay down their weapons and return to their homes. The fort was empty and undefended.

Little Pierre had just brought Captain Leonard Helm of the American army to Captain Bousseron's office. The American was not happy. Pierre did not leave Bousseron's office after fetching the American there. He simply sat down in a chair in a dark corner of the room and listened to the two arguing officers. The men didn't seem to notice that he was still there.

Captain Helm almost screamed at Bousseron. "A fine bunch of soldiers you Frenchmen turned out to be! Your men tucked their tails and ran home the moment they heard the word, 'British!'"

Captain Bousseron pleaded, "You must understand, Leonard. They had no other choice!"

"That's a lie!" bellowed Helm. "You and your men could stand with us and fight!"

"Stand with who? The three of you? And with only one small cannon? Don't you understand Hamilton's threat? This is not some faraway battlefield. This fort stands only a few hundred yards from our homes! Our wives and our children and grandchildren are just a short distance down the street."

Captain Bousseron paused and gathered his thoughts.

"Leonard, the British have threatened to unleash their Indians upon us. You know what that means! They would slay and scalp every Frenchman in this town. They would burn and utterly destroy our homes and our village. There is no way that these local men could be expected to resist such a powerful force of enemy soldiers!"

"Yes, they could, Captain! Courage is a choice. Cowering down and running from a fight is a choice. And it seems that your men have already made their choice. There aren't a dozen Frenchmen left inside the walls of this fort. The rest of them have melted into the darkness and are now hiding under the skirts of their women!"

"Tell me … what would you do if this were your home, Leonard?"

"Excuse me?" responded Captain Helm.

"I said … what would you do if Vincennes were your home? What would you do if your wife and children were sleeping in a house down the street?"

"That has nothing to do with the matter at hand," retorted Helm.

"It has everything to do with it!" shrieked Bousseron. "That is the true issue here! My men are loyal. They want your liberty and freedom. They are willing to pay a very high price, but not at the expense of their families and homes!"

"Your people owe me, Francois!"

"Owe you?" shrieked Bousseron in disbelief. "You think we owe you? That is insane! You owe us! You certainly owe me! Since you and your men arrived here all that you have done is eat our food and play cards. The businesses in Vincennes have cash drawers full of worthless receipts from you and from Virginia. If your government some day does not pay me, I will be financially ruined! That is how dedicated we citizens of Vincennes are to the American cause! But, again I say, we will not sacrifice our women and children to the war clubs and knives of Hamilton's Indians."

Helm grunted his disdain. "I still say that you're all a bunch of cowardly, half-hearted traitors."

"Well, I'm still standing here, aren't I, Leonard? Am I not demonstrating my dedication to your cause?"

Helm paused and stared at Bousseron. "I suppose so. But what do we do now? We only have a dozen men left."

"I do not know," replied a frustrated Captain Bousseron. "We must think, and quickly."

"We can hide everything," chirped Pierre from the corner.

Both men's heads spun around as they stared in the direction of Pierre's voice.

"Has that lad been here the entire time?" demanded Captain Helm.

Captain Bousseron shook his head in disbelief. "I suppose so. Pierre, why are you still here? I thought you left after you summoned Captain Helm."

"No, sir. You never told me to leave."

"No, I suppose I didn't. But still, you should not be here." The captain paused and looked inquisitively at Pierre. "What are you talking about? What must we hide?"

"Everything. Powder, lead, food … anything the British might need. Some of the men of the village are already doing it. The father of one of my friends has already hidden all of his furs, lead, and gunpowder. He says that lead and powder will be the things they will try to take first."

Captain Bousseron turned and stared thoughtfully into the dancing, orange fire inside his tiny fireplace. Pierre could see that he was genuinely considering his suggestion.

Bousseron spun around excitedly. "Leonard, the boy is right! We need to get all of the powder and lead out of the fort and hide it in the village."

"Hide it? Where?"

"We can bury it. I know of a couple of good places. We can also take all of the food, equipment, and other supplies and distribute them among the households of the village. The people will hide those, as well. The less that we leave inside this fort for the British, the less comfortable and harsher their winter will be. We can recover the gunpowder and supplies when Colonel Clark returns to attack the fort in the spring."

"Where will you hide everything?"

Bousseron paused. "I think it's best that you do not know. We would not want the British to interrogate you and find out, would we?"

The American nodded. "You're right, Francois. It is best that I do not know. The secret will be yours. You must proceed immediately. We do not have a moment to spare."

"Very well, Captain Helm. I will have this fort cleaned out and all provisions concealed before dawn."

The men shook hands. Captain Helm smiled. "Thank you, Francois. I am truly sorry for the angry things I said to you."

Captain Bousseron bowed slightly and then made his way toward the exit. "I understand your frustration, Leonard." He snapped his fingers at Pierre. "Come along, son. We have work to do."

Little Pierre jumped to his feet and followed his captain toward the door.

CHAPTER EIGHT
INVADERS AND PRISONERS

The British soldiers arrived about an hour after daybreak. There were approximately sixty men in their invasion force. Amazingly, most of the soldiers were actually Frenchmen from Canada. The soldiers grounded their canoes and then spread out along the riverbank before moving toward the village and fort.

Vincennes was curiously silent. There was not a soul to be seen in the streets, shops, or businesses. The only movement within the town was the occasional chicken, dog, or goat that wandered across the otherwise deserted streets. The windows and doors of every home and business were shuttered and silent. There was no sign of life.

Little Pierre had found the perfect hiding place. He lay concealed beneath a huge spruce tree that stood beside the Catholic Church. The bottom branches of the enormous evergreen tree reached all the way to the ground, forming a dense thicket of heavy green needles. Behind those limbs, however, the tree was like a big, open cave. The ground beneath its limbs was clear.

Pierre had a perfect vantage point to observe the action in front of the fort. It was an ideal hideout. The other members of the band of young spies were similarly hidden throughout the town.

The enemy soldiers were spooked by the absolute quiet inside the town. The commander of the British force was an officer dressed in a beautiful red and gold uniform and a large, black cocked hat. He stepped forward into the street and placed himself in full view of the fort and most of the nearby homes. The huge ostrich feather that stuck out of the top of his hat bobbed in the air as he shouted loudly toward the town.

"Citizens of Vincennes! I am Major Jehu Hay of the army of Great Britain! I come from Detroit in the name of His Majesty King George III and his worthy representative, the honorable Lieutenant Governor Henry Hamilton! We have come today to liberate this village and its people from the occupation by the rebels of Virginia! Is there a representative of the people of the village willing to step forward for conference and parley?"

Just a few yards away a door opened at the village store and a tall, distinguished young man stepped out and ambled into the street. He was dressed in a gray and white blanket capote trimmed with a dull red stripe. Fresh, clean buckskin leggings with antler buttons showed beneath the coat. He wore thick, fur-lined moccasins on his feet. On his head he wore a bright red wool cap with the word, "*Liberté*," the French word for "Liberty," embroidered in white across the brow.

It was Captain Francois Bousseron. He waved at Major Hay in a friendly manner and smiled broadly to demonstrate his lack of hostile intent. He could see that at least a dozen muskets were aimed at him.

Captain Bousseron walked to within ten feet of the British officer, stopped, and bowed slightly. "Major Hay, I am Francois Bousseron, captain of the militia and mayor of this village."

"Then you are authorized to speak for the people?"

"Absolutely, Major. I am the elected spokesman for all citizens of Vincennes, and I come to ease any fears that you may have regarding our intentions."

The major glared at the Frenchman with a look of confidence and pride. "I am not sure whether to be encouraged or offended by the message written on your cap, sir."

Bousseron smiled wryly. "Indeed, Major. Well, you may interpret my cap however you wish. But believe me when I say that we have no intentions of resisting your army. We received the dispatch from Governor Hamilton yesterday and have responded as he demanded. The vast majority of the men of Vincennes have laid down their arms and returned to their homes and families."

"Majority?" questioned the Major.

"Yes, Major. A few men remain inside the fort with the Americans."

"How many?" demanded the major.

"Perhaps a dozen or so. The remainder are concealed within their homes."

"And do the men in their homes still have their muskets?"

"Of course. They will need them for hunting and feeding their families."

Major Hay nodded. "I understand. We would never deprive the men of Vincennes of the ability to provide meat for their families."

Captain Bousseron bowed respectfully to the major. "Then, Major Hay, I hereby offer you our surrender and declare that the town is yours. I implore you not to unleash your Indians upon our people. We have complied with your governor's demands."

"He is your governor now, as well," Major Hay corrected him.

Bousseron nodded in submission. He appealed to the British officer, "Might I make an inquiry, Major?"

"Of course, Captain."

"Several of my men are missing. I dispatched them on a patrol to the north two weeks ago and we have not heard from them in several days. Did your party encounter these men?"

Major Hay nodded. "Yes. Our forward scouts captured your patrol two days ago. They are in custody and in good health. We brought them with us this morning, and they are under guard near our boats."

"That is good news, Major. We were very concerned that they had fallen upon some grave misfortune."

"As I said, your men are well. It is our intention to release them to you once we are established in the fort … all except one."

"Excuse me?" asked a confused Captain Bousseron.

"One of the prisoners is under sentence of death. It is the leader of the group, Sergeant Pierre Grimard."

"Why, on earth, is Sergeant Grimard under such a sentence? What has he done?"

"Governor Hamilton has sentenced him to hang on the charge of murder. I cannot comment further."

"Murder?" exploded the captain. "Who did he murder?"

"I am not at liberty to discuss the situation with you, Captain!" snapped Major Hay. "It is a matter for the Crown. Now, if you would please return to your home, as well. I will fetch you if I need you. I must send for the governor and prepare to take the fort."

"But, Major …"

"That is all, Captain. You are dismissed. Please go away."

Major Hay turned his back to Bousseron and focused his attention on the fort. Captain Bousseron turned and trotted quickly down the street toward the Grimard home.

Little Pierre, still concealed beneath the large tree, could not hear the words spoken by the two men. They were too far away from him. But after their conversation Pierre saw Captain Bousseron run down the street and enter the gate to his own home.

Pierre quickly backed his way out from under the tree, ran around behind the church, and sprinted into the alley behind his home. He had to get there quickly and find out what was happening!

Pierre ran through the door of his house just in time to hear his mother scream. It was a horrible, heartbroken sound. Pierre was confused.

"Murder? They've charged him with murder?" screeched Genevieve in disbelief.

The woman was standing near the fireplace. The combination of cold winter air and disturbing news caused her to be a bit light-headed. She placed her hand on the mantle to steady herself.

"Who, in God's name, is my husband supposed to have murdered?" she mumbled as she stared at the glowing coals. "The entire notion is preposterous. Something must have gone horribly wrong on that patrol." She snapped a look of despair at Bousseron. "Francois, you know Pierre better than most of the men in this village. Surely you know that he is not capable of murder."

"The British major would not give me any other details. He simply said that Lieutenant Governor Henry Hamilton had issued the sentence of death for the crime of murder."

Genevieve's head spun when she heard that name … Henry Hamilton. She hissed, "Are you sure that is the name that he said?"

"I am certain … Henry Hamilton."

Her chin dropped to her chest. She took a deep breath and then looked into the captain's eyes. "I know that man. Pierre knows him, as well."

"How could you possibly know a British governor from Detroit?" exclaimed Bousseron.

She answered, "We encountered him during our journey up the Mississippi River almost ten years ago. During a brief stopover at a British fort on the river there was an English soldier who picked a fight with

Pierre. My husband had to defend himself. He was forced to draw his pistol and fire. The soldier died."

"But that was so long ago!" protested the captain.

She replied, "Yes, it was. Henry Hamilton wanted Pierre executed that very night. The British governor at the post found him innocent of any wrongdoing and released him. We left the next morning. I believe that Hamilton was very insulted and his pride was wounded deeply."

"And so, you think that this Governor Hamilton somehow recognized Pierre and now intends on following through with what he wanted to do ten years ago?"

"There can be no other explanation. It cannot be a coincidence that Henry Hamilton is leading this expedition that now holds my husband as a captive."

Bousseron whistled and shook his head in disbelief.

Little Pierre stood petrified near the door. He could not believe what he had just heard. He was frantic with worry and fear. He threw open the door and ran outside.

"Pierre! Wait!" his mother yelled. "Come back this instant!"

But it was too late. The lad had already jumped the fence and was running in the direction of the fort.

"Let him go, Genevieve. He is upset and needs to find some friends to console him."

"But the British!" she protested.

"Do not worry. Not even the British are evil enough to make war against little boys. Little Pierre will be just fine."

Pierre disappeared for the remainder of the day. Unbeknownst to his mother, he spent the entire afternoon organizing his little band of spies and gathering information on the British. His mother was worried sick about him. He loudly burst through the door of the Grimard house just as the evening sun descended below the horizon. He was breathless and excited.

"I saw him, Mama! I saw him!"

His mother was hovering over a pot beside the mantle and tasting a stew that she had prepared for supper. She turned and placed both hands on her hips and began to scold the boy. "Pierre Grimard, where have you been all the long day? I have been worried sick about you! There are enemy soldiers all over this town! I thought for sure that one of them had captured you!"

"You are not listening to me, Mama. I saw him! I saw Papa!"

She ran to him and placed her hands on his shoulders. There was a glint of hope in her eyes.

"Where, Pierre? Where did you see him?"

"They brought him up from the river about an hour ago. I saw Mr. Turpin and the others, as well. The British released them, but they took Papa into the fort."

"So then … the fort has surrendered?" she asked.

"Yes, Mama. No one fired a shot. I saw the tall American go out and talk to two British men." His face became dark and grim. "I heard him call one of them, 'Governor Hamilton.'"

Genevieve bit her lip nervously. "Well, at least it is over now. Thank God they did not unleash the Indians upon our village."

"I don't think they plan to, Mama. The Indians plundered and took lots of things from the fort. After they were done I saw most of them get into canoes and paddle back upriver. All that remains in the fort now are British and some Frenchmen they brought with them from Canada. There might be a handful of Indians, but not many."

She nodded her understanding. "So, you saw Governor Henry Hamilton with your own eyes? He is here in Vincennes?"

"Yes, Mama."

Genevieve was trembling. "Did you see where they took your father?"

He shook his head. "No, Mama. But he was most definitely being held prisoner. His hands were tied together in front of him."

A single tear crept down her cheek. "Was he injured?"

"I do not think so. I saw no blood. He appeared to be in good spirits. He walked with strength and pride." Young Pierre smiled proudly, himself.

"Why have you waited so long to come home and tell me?" she scolded the boy. "I have been sick to death for news!"

"Because I was hiding, Mama. I was concealed on top of Mr. Pineau's shed. I had to wait until their patrols went in for the night before I could come down. The fort is locked up tight now. I do not think anyone will be going in or out until morning."

His mother smiled slightly at him and then tousled his light brown hair. "You are a brave boy, Pierre. Just like your father. Our very own little spy of Vincennes."

She turned and walked toward the fireplace. "Come and get some stew and bread in your belly. I know that you must be hungry. After you eat you need to go and report what you have seen to Captain Bousseron."

Pierre smiled sheepishly. "Mama, I went to see him before I came home. He said that he would be here in about an hour. He had to meet someone else first before coming here to make a plan."

"Make a plan?" she asked, confused.

"Yes, Mama. A plan to get Papa out of that fort."

CHAPTER NINE
A VERY REAL SPY MISSION

Captain Bousseron raised his voice. He did not shout, but he spoke with great force and conviction. "Genevieve, this is the only way!"

She shook her head vigorously. "I cannot allow you to use my son in your plans. I may have already lost my husband. I will not sacrifice his oldest son to set him free."

"But I know that it will work, Genevieve! It is a simple, foolproof plan. We will get Pierre out of his British imprisonment, but first we need to know where he is. We need intelligence from inside the walls of the fort."

Genevieve, ever the overprotective mother, shook her head in protest. "I cannot send my boy into a fort occupied by the British and their allies on a spy mission! What if he is caught? What if he is arrested? No! No! I simply cannot allow it."

Little Pierre's young voice echoed from a dark corner of the cabin near the fireplace. "I can do it, Mama. It sounds easy. I will just deliver dinner for Papa on Sunday, let him know that we are all just fine, and find out exactly where they are holding him. I will also try to see what changes the British are making to the inside of the fort. Afterwards I will come right back home and make my report to the captain."

Bousseron added, "Father Gibault has already agreed to the plan, Genevieve. He will accompany the boy. He will enter the fort on Sunday in order to administer the Holy Communion to the soldiers and prisoners. The priest will serve as escort for little Pierre and secure permission for him to deliver a hot meal to your husband. The entire visit should take no more than an hour at most."

"Why do you not enter the fort and see Pierre, yourself? He is, after all, a soldier under your command," challenged Genevieve somewhat spitefully.

"My dear, they will not allow me into their fort! They consider me to be something of a traitor to their cause. Which I am, by the way!" He winked at little Pierre. The boy smiled. "It will be some time before I will earn enough of Hamilton's trust to be given access to their fort."

"Then I, myself, will take him his meal! I will find out what you need to know!"

Bousseron shook his head vigorously. "No, Genevieve. That fort is no place for a young woman. Besides, like you just told me, you and Pierre have some bad history with Hamilton. He may remember you. No, Genevieve. I will not place you in such a dangerous situation."

"But you will place my boy in danger?" she responded in disbelief.

"Your boy has already proven his worth to our cause. He was able to move throughout this entire town undetected today. As a child he enjoys a degree of invisibility. Besides, the lad wants to help his father! He is a very capable and worthy spy. No one would suspect a young boy," Bousseron pleaded passionately.

Genevieve buried her face in her hands as she agonized over the entire situation. Her nerves were shattered. She was a very frightened woman. She was physically exhausted. She was barely a month away from giving birth to another child. Her husband was in British bondage and headed for the gallows. And to top it all off her nine-year-old son was eager to act as a spy and perform a secret mission on behalf of the French militia!

Francois Bousseron spoke quietly and respectfully. "Genevieve … I need your permission. I will not proceed without it. We have precious little time to make all of the arrangements."

Pierre rose from his chair and walked over to her. He placed his arm reassuringly around her shoulder and rested his cheek on the top of her head.

"Mama, it will be all right. I promise you it will. I am not afraid. I will be brave." He cupped her chin with his hand and turned her face toward him. "I have to do this, Mama. I do not want you to go anywhere near those bad men. Please let me go. Please let me help Papa."

Genevieve wiped the tears from her face and embraced her son. After a short while she released him and then rose from her bench. She walked over and peeked through the privacy curtains at the far end of the cabin. Beyond the thin cloth both of her younger sons slept peacefully on the floor on their shared feather mattress. She closed her eyes and uttered a silent prayer. She turned and faced the militia commander.

"All right, Francois. Pierre will be your spy. Now … what must I do?"

Francois grinned broadly. "You merely need to cook your husband a delicious dinner. What do you think he would like? Venison or beef?"

The gates of Fort Sackville stood open. Four French-Canadian militiamen stood vigilant guard nearby. Father Gibault shuffled toward the entrance to the fort. The hem of his brown robe hovered just above the muddy ground. His very large belly jiggled with each step. He carried with him a basket containing a small bottle of wine, a round loaf of communion bread, and a gold drinking cup. Pierre walked one step behind him. The boy carried a rather large basket of food covered with a pale brown linen cloth.

They were a mere ten steps from the fort when one of the Frenchmen confronted them. "Stop! I am sorry, Father, but you may proceed no further."

"Surely, my child, you will not inhibit the work of a servant of the Lord," pleaded Father Gibault. "What is your name, boy?"

The young soldier seemed somewhat ashamed. "Alain Dupuis, Father. I apologize, sincerely, but citizens of the village are not allowed inside the fort under any circumstances. Major Hay's orders."

"My son, I have come to administer the Sacrament of Holy Communion to the men of this fort. Today is the Sabbath day, after all. It is my responsibility to minister to the men here, no matter their nationality or political allegiances."

The soldier's eyes lit up. "We have not received communion for over three months, Father."

Father Gibault shook his head in an exaggerated gesture of shock and shame. "Just as I suspected. Your commanders departed Detroit without tending to the spiritual needs of their men. I did not even see a humble Brother or Friar among your troops."

The soldier nodded. "It is true, Father. And a shame it is, too. There are many Frenchmen here who would be most grateful for communion."

"So, we have ourselves something of a dilemma, do we not? I come to provide the ministry, but your commander will not allow me inside the fort. Do you think, perhaps, that we could make a small exception and beg for special permission for me to enter?"

"What is the boy's purpose in being here?" inquired the soldier.

"He is merely here to assist me. I have received word that there is a man from Vincennes being held inside the fort under sentence of death. I have brought that condemned man a hot, satisfying meal."

"Yes, there is a man sentenced to hang on Christmas Day, but I am not sure that the major will allow any special treatment on his behalf."

"Might you summon an officer, perhaps even Major Hay, himself, so that I can appeal my case directly to his authority?" pleaded Father Gibault.

"Of course, Father. I will fetch someone immediately."

The militiaman turned and gave brief instructions to his men and then walked quickly into the fort. He followed a path toward the commander's office. Several minutes later he returned with a British officer.

"I am Major Jehu Hay, commander of the military forces of Vincennes and Fort Sackville. The sergeant has explained to me that you have come to administer Holy Communion to the men."

"That is, indeed, the truth, Major. I would count it an honor to hold Mass and administer the Sacrament to my brethren within your ranks."

"Are you the priest who regularly serves this village?"

"I am, sir. I am well-known by all the residents here, having baptized most of their children. Any one of them can offer testimony to my office and ministry in the Holy Catholic Church."

The major exhaled slightly and considered the request. He looked judiciously into the priest's eyes.

"I suppose that your administration of communion would be acceptable to me, Father. What about this boy? What is his purpose in being here?"

"You are holding a member of my church under sentence of death, Major. One of the women of our town has prepared him a hot meal. I invited this child to carry the basket and deliver it to the man."

The major raised an eyebrow. "He is a member of your church?"

"Yes, Major. Everyone knows that you are holding Pierre Grimard and that he is to be hanged. No one questions your authority to do so. We would merely like to minister to our brother until such time as the unthinkable sentence is carried out."

"I suppose there is no harm in that," responded the major. "Sergeant Grimard seems like a decent fellow. I am certain that he would enjoy the visit and the meal. We will, of course, have to inspect the contents of the basket."

"Of course, Major. You will discover that it is merely a bowl of venison stew, some slices of fresh bread, a small pie, and some wine."

"My man will examine the basket and then escort the boy to the blockhouse where the prisoner is being detained. You may set up your altar near the main office. I will notify the garrison of your availability."

"Thank you. You are most gracious, Major." Father Gibault nodded respectfully.

"And you are most welcome, Father," responded the major. "Sergeant, please check the boy's basket and then escort him to the prisoner's quarters."

"Yes, Major!"

The sergeant of the French militia flipped back the linen cover on little Pierre's basket and examined the contents quickly. He seemed satisfied that they were safe enough.

The sergeant mumbled, "Come with me, son."

Pierre walked obediently beside the strange, bearded Canadian. As he walked he scanned in every direction within the fort. Men were working feverishly throughout the post, repairing the palisades and building lookout positions high on the walls. Some were even building new buildings that looked like houses along the southern edge of the compound. Pierre made a mental note of it all so that he could make a thorough report to Captain Bousseron.

The sergeant inquired quietly, "Do you know this man to whom you are delivering the food?"

Pierre answered honestly, "He is my father."

The Frenchman grinned. "I suspected as much. I thought that I noticed a resemblance." Pierre looked up at the man, who winked at him in return. "I will allow you to visit with your father for a nice, long while. It will be our secret … one Frenchman doing another a favor."

Pierre nodded and smiled.

It took a couple of minutes for them to cross the compound. The man guided little Pierre toward a corner blockhouse. It was the structure nearest the Wabash River. When they reached the door, the guard pulled back the heavy iron latch and cracked the door to look inside at the elder Pierre Grimard. His face showed his pity for his fellow Frenchman being held prisoner.

"I will give you as much time as I possibly can with your father. It may be the last time you ever see him, so make the most of it. I am very sorry."

He pushed the door open all the way and encouraged Pierre to step across the log threshold. It took a moment for the boy's eyes to adjust to the darkness inside. Then he saw the dark outline of a body lying against the wall to his right.

"Papa!"

His father raised up slowly onto one elbow. He stared in disbelief at his son. Little Pierre placed the basket on the ground and ran toward his father just as the heavy timber door slammed shut behind him.

"Pierre! My boy! How did you get here?"

Pierre tumbled into his father's arms and hugged him tight.

CHAPTER TEN
PIERRE HAS A PLAN

"And you are certain this is where he is being held?" inquired Captain Bousseron, pointing at his crude, hand-drawn map.

The captain and all of the other people in the room stared intently at young Pierre. In addition to Bousseron, the meeting included Father Gibault, Genevieve Grimard, and two of Bousseron's loyal militia lieutenants.

Little Pierre nodded vigorously. "I am certain, Captain. It is the blockhouse that is to the left rear of the compound when you enter through the main gate. It is right along the river. You can even hear the sounds of the moving water from inside his room."

Lieutenant Oscar Hamelin added, "Father Gibault said that the British are improving the defenses of the fort. Did you notice that, as well?"

"Yes, sir. There were dozens of men hard at work on the buildings and fort walls. They were sealing several wide places between the logs. One group of men was even building a series of small buildings along the wall on the western side."

The lieutenant looked grimly at Bousseron and said one word. "Barracks."

"Indeed," responded Bousseron. "Our British friends are preparing themselves for a long, cold winter."

A frustrated Genevieve Grimard interrupted their military discussion. "That is all quite interesting, gentlemen, but what are you planning to do to free my husband? I care nothing about your talk of walls and barracks. They plan to hang my Pierre in five days!"

"That corner blockhouse is thirty yards from the rear gate. It is a long way to move in the open, even under cover of darkness," remarked Lieutenant Hamelin.

"The new barracks are very close. I doubt that it would even be a possibility to enter the gate and reach the door of the blockhouse unseen," stated Bousseron. "We must think differently."

"What are you saying?" inquired Father Gibault. "How else could we possibly get him out if not through a gate?"

"I do not know!" exclaimed Bousseron, slamming his fist on the table. "I have absolutely no ideas! But we must do something! I cannot stand the notion of these uppity Redcoats hanging my friend!"

The men stared in frustration at their map of the fort. The room became silent.

Little Pierre's high-pitched voice interrupted the silence. "What about that old shed down by the river?"

"What old shed?" demanded Bousseron.

"There is a very old, broken down shed between the fort and the river. Part of it has fallen down completely … the section closest to the water. That part was washed out by floodwaters, but most of it is still standing. I have never seen the building used for anything. I think it was there even before they built the fort."

"I have neither seen nor heard of such a structure," retorted the captain.

"You cannot see it from the fort. It is in that thick cluster of big cedar and pine trees right beside the corner blockhouse. But I have played in it for years. We children like to pretend that it is our own secret fortress."

Bousseron responded, "I know about the cluster of trees, but I was unaware of any building. Still, I do not see what use that information is to us, Pierre. Your father is imprisoned inside the fort walls. A shack beside the river is useless in our situation."

"We can dig him out," Pierre announced with confidence. "We can dig a tunnel from the shack."

His words lingered dramatically in the dark, cold room. The adults tried to envision the execution of Pierre's outlandish idea.

"That is impossible," responded Lieutenant David Aubin, another of Bousseron's officers. "The distance is too great, and we would be discovered."

The little boy pointed at the map. "But it is not even twenty-five feet to the wall." He grinned. "Besides, we have already started the digging for you."

"Whatever do you mean, Pierre?" demanded his mother.

"We started digging a tunnel just for fun way back last winter. We were going to try to get into the fort and cause a little mischief among the British troops. We got about half-way to the wall but the sides kept crumbling."

"Good Lord!" his mother shouted.

The boy pleaded innocently, "It is all right, Mama. We stopped as soon as the dirt started giving way. No one was hurt."

"Only by the grace of God!" she barked at him.

Bousseron interrupted the mother-son argument. "I think the boy is onto something." He looked to his lieutenants. "David, we could use the scrap lumber from the building to shore up the sides and roof of a tunnel. If what Pierre tells us is true, we only need to dig another ten to fifteen feet to reach inside the wall. The building is already well out of view. After all, none of us have ever even seen it! We could sneak into the shed under cover of darkness and have our men dig night and day."

Lieutenant Hamelin's eyes widened. "We could even reach that spot by canoe if we need to. And we could toss the loose dirt into the river and simply let it wash away!" He looked with renewed confidence at his commander. "It might work!"

Bousseron grinned and slapped a happy hand on the tabletop. "Yes, it will work! We begin tonight! We only have four days to dig a tunnel to free our fellow compatriot." He playfully tapped his fist against Pierre's chin. "Let us see if we can get inside those walls and cause some mischief. Eh, Pierre?"

The boy beamed with pride and pleasure.

Captain Bousseron had joined the daytime shift of tunnel diggers in the pre-dawn darkness. It was Christmas Eve. Pierre Grimard was scheduled to be hanged at noon on Christmas Day. Some rough gallows had been completed just outside the main gate of the fort. Governor Hamilton had already issued a summons to all citizens of Vincennes. He expected every man, woman, and child of the village to attend the execution of this enemy of the Crown. Bousseron knew that his men were working against the clock. He wanted to personally check on their progress.

The men had worked diligently for three days and nights. Eighteen men volunteered to take part in digging the tunnel. The men progressed steadily over the three-day time period. They believed that they had dug enough to be exactly under Pierre's cell, so they called in Captain Bousseron to measure and verify their progress. He crawled inside the tunnel with a length of string and a small candle. Several minutes later he emerged from the tunnel and measured his string. It totaled just over twenty-seven feet.

Captain Bousseron grinned and then whispered, "That is it, gentlemen. We are beneath his room!"

"What do we do now, Captain?"

"We dig no further. But we need to widen the spot at the end of the tunnel. It needs to be a slightly larger box so that a man can drop down from above and turn his body in order to move toward the exit. That is your job for today. But do not dig upward! Pierre does not know that we are coming, yet. We must inform him today. Tonight we will dig up through the floor and get him out of there. Excellent work, men!"

The captain shook the hands of the three tunnelers and then donned his hat, coat, and bags and scurried out of the old shack. He made his way quietly through the thick trees toward the south and then circled around the outskirts of the village and entered Vincennes from the northeast. He headed straight for the Grimard home.

"I do not make this request lightly, Francois," replied Genevieve, her voice firm and her chin held high. "I should take the final meal to Pierre. His captors will think it odd that his wife has not been to see him during his imprisonment. They will be doubly suspicious if I do not go to see him this afternoon."

"But Genevieve, I still do not like the notion of you going inside that fort."

"You worry too much, Francois. Father Gibault will accompany me, as well as my boys. We need to make the British believe that we have accepted his execution. They will expect that his family would visit him before he goes to the gallows."

"She is right, Francois," chimed in Father Gibault. "We need to keep the British distracted and not even entertaining the notion of a possible escape. They will, most certainly, expect his family to visit him today. I will make all of the necessary arrangements."

Captain Bousseron inhaled deeply, shifting his gaze between the priest and Genevieve. "Do you think you can convince them of your despair? How good of an actor are you?"

Genevieve sported a devilish grin. "Oh, they will believe me, Francois. I will become a wailing, emotional, hysterical wife. They will enjoy the show."

Captain Bousseron chuckled. Father Gibault smiled mischievously.

CHAPTER ELEVEN
ESCAPE!

The family made their way slowly across the compound. The mud inside the fort was thick and sticky. Father Gibault supported Genevieve as best he could. She wailed and cried every step that she took across the fort grounds. He soon found himself unable to support her weight.

"Sergeant, can you please assist me?" he implored the French militiaman walking beside them.

"Of course, Father." The soldier reached and took hold of Genevieve's other arm.

The woman wailed even more ferociously when the strange man touched her. The younger boys, Charles and Jean-Baptiste, both cried, as well. They didn't know why they were crying. The fact that their mother was so upset was enough to bring them to tears.

Pierre marched proudly beside the two adults. He carried his father's "final" meal in a beautifully decorated basket. The French guards had inspected it diligently, but were careful not to disturb the contents. The two younger boys each carried a wool blanket. The guards inspected them, as well.

The French guards were very respectful of the emotional, mourning family. Father Gibault noticed tears in their eyes. Clearly, the Canadian Frenchmen were not in favor of the execution of one of their distant countrymen. The Father smiled within his heart, for he knew that their ruse was working.

As they neared the blockhouse the guard released Genevieve to Father Gibault's grip and reached into his leather bag to retrieve a large key. He stuck the key into an enormous lock that hung on a newly forged iron latch.

As the French guard opened the door he mumbled to Genevieve, "Madame, I will secure the gate in one hour. You may have that much time to spend with your husband. I will come and fetch you before we close the fort for the night."

Genevieve and Father Gibault nodded. Just as they were about to enter the cell another Frenchman approached them with a lighted candle lantern. The tall candle glowed brightly inside its glass casing. In his other hand he carried a small three-legged stool.

The man bowed as he handed the lantern to Genevieve. "Madame, you will need this lantern. It is very dark inside the room. And you will need this stool to sit upon, as well. I assume that your boys can all sit on the floor." He smiled glumly at the forlorn woman and handed the stool to Father Gibault.

Genevieve wiped her ample tears and snotty nose with a linen handkerchief as she muttered, "Thank you, sir. Your kindness will not be forgotten."

Father Gibault escorted Genevieve into the blockhouse. The boys followed. After the heavy timber door slammed shut behind them an emotional family reunion began to take place inside the dark, low-ceilinged room.

A deep, congested cough gurgled in the darkness. Pierre's weak voice mumbled from the far corner, "Genevieve? My love! Is that you? Or is it an angel that has come to visit me and take me on to heaven?" He coughed another deep, thunderous cough.

"It is I, husband. And I have brought your boys."

The two youngest lads screamed, "Papa!" as they swarmed their father. The youngsters embraced him and showered him with kisses.

"Oh, my boys! My boys! My boys! I am so glad to see you! I have missed you so!"

"Papa, you have big whiskers," teased Charles, giggling.

"I grew them to tickle your skinny little neck, Master Charles." He grabbed the boy and buried his chin beneath the lad's soft neck, causing him to emit a delighted squeal.

Tears filled the man's eyes. He struggled to stand.

"Do not try to get up, Pierre. Stay where you are. Conserve your strength. We will join you, instead," encouraged Father Gibault.

The priest placed the stool next to the wall beside Pierre and helped Genevieve get seated comfortably beside her husband. Pierre draped his arm across her lap and buried his face into her side. He wept openly and without shame.

"My darling, I have missed you so much that it hurts." His tears flowed. He coughed.

Genevieve stroked her husband's stringy hair and wept with him. She felt of his forehead. "Oh, my Lord! You have a high fever! I need to get you home and take care of you properly. This cold has moved into your bones and afflicted your throat and chest."

Pierre removed his face from his wife's soft, fragrant dress and wiped his cheeks with his sleeves. He took hold of his wife's tiny hand. He coughed again, deeply.

"How I wish that were possible, my love. But you and I both know the injustice that confronts us in the morning. I have heard the gallows being built outside the gate. I have endured the teasing and taunting of my British captors. They plan to hang me tomorrow at noon. There is no escape for me. See … my son has brought me my last meal. Come here, Pierre."

The solemn boy walked over to his father, leaned down, and gently hugged him. He kissed his papa's cheek. Pierre grabbed his son and pulled him close and tight.

"How is my big boy? Have you been taking care of your mother?"

"Yes, Papa. Mama says that I have been an excellent 'man of the house.'"

Pierre chuckled and hugged his son again.

"You must have faith, my son, that you will be delivered," declared the priest, interrupting the father-son embrace.

"My faith has escaped me, Father. I see no other possible outcome for me. I am afraid that you will bury me in your churchyard before sundown tomorrow."

Father Gibault leaned closer and whispered, "I do not think so, Pierre. In fact, I quite expect that you will be far away from Vincennes before dusk on our Lord's birthday." The priest's eyes gleamed with mischief and joy. His face erupted into a wide, plump grin.

Pierre glanced at Genevieve. He could see her equally huge smile in the warm glow of the lone candle.

"What is he talking about, Genevieve?"

She leaned toward him and took his chin in her hand. She hissed quietly, "We are breaking you out of this prison tonight, my love."

"What? How?" Pierre exclaimed a bit too loudly.

Father Gibault threw his finger up to his lips. "Shhhh! There are curious ears beyond these walls."

Now Pierre was excited. He felt new energy creeping into his limbs. He scrambled onto his knees.

"Tell me … what is going on?" He coughed again.

Father Gibault nodded at Genevieve.

Genevieve whispered into his ear, "Captain Bousseron and his men are getting you out tonight. They have tunneled beneath the wall and have reached a point directly underneath this room. Tonight after dark they will dig upward to reach you and set you free."

Pierre's eyes grew wide with disbelief. He stared at the floor. "They are under this room?"

"Yes, Pierre," responded the priest. "At this very moment. They started from beneath an old shack just beyond the wall. It is a secret place down by the river." He paused. "It was all little Pierre's idea."

Pierre glanced proudly at his son. "Is that so?"

The boy glowed with pride. He nodded silently at his father.

Pierre whispered to his wife, "What happens once I am free?"

"The men will have a canoe hidden at the river's edge beyond the shed. Thick brush, pine trees, and cedar trees conceal the entire area very well. Your canoe will be stocked with extra clothing, blankets, food, and weapons. You must go south on the river and then make your way west to Kaskaskia and the protection of the Virginians."

Again, tears began to flow down Pierre's tired, filthy cheeks. He simply could not believe the news that his family had brought to him. His joy was quickly overshadowed by a series of violent coughing spasms.

He managed to get out a single question through the coughing. "When will they come?"

"Late tonight, after the garrison is bedded down. That will give you several hours head start on the river before sunrise. You will be well beyond their reach by dawn and will leave no trail," answered Father Gibault.

Pierre whispered, "I am so excited, I do not think I will be able to eat this fine meal!"

His wife tenderly pushed back the hair from his eyes. "You must eat, Pierre. You need strength. I have a small jar of rum, and I have some fragrant salve in my bag. I will coat your neck and chest with the ointment. The aroma should help loosen up that horrid cough."

Father Gibault assumed his priestly authority. "Before you eat, my son, we will pray for your meal, and for your health, and for our little conspiracy. And then you can eat while your family catches you up on all of their latest news. Afterwards, when we leave, Genevieve and the children will have to wail and cry with convincing despair and emotion. We need the British to hear how brokenhearted you all are about Pierre's appointment with the gallows tomorrow. Do you all think you can do that?"

Every member of the family grinned and nodded vigorously.

"Good!" responded the priest. "Now, let us pray."

Pierre was finally warm. The moist cold of the blockhouse had been torturous for the past week, but his two new blankets provided him with a cocoon of luxurious warmth. At first Pierre found it difficult to sleep. He was too excited. Even as he slumbered fitfully he continued to awaken and glance around the room, searching for any sign of his rescuers. After almost an hour of tossing and turning he finally faced the wall and surrendered to a deep, restful sleep.

Then he felt his leg shaking.

A voice hissed in the darkness, "Pierre!"

He thought he was dreaming until he received a harsh slap on the shoulder.

"Pierre! Wake up! It is time to go!"

He rolled over onto his back and stared into a very familiar and unexpected face in the darkness. It was his good friend, neighbor, and compatriot Francois Turpin.

"Francois! I cannot believe it is you!"

Pierre tossed his blankets aside and embraced his friend.

"I am not alone, Pierre. I have a brave assistant with me."

Pierre looked over the man's shoulder and saw his son, little Pierre, hovering beside the escape hole. Tears of pride filled the man's eyes.

"Come quickly, Papa. We have no time to waste. The tunnel is over here beside the fireplace. We barely made it into the room, but we made it. Close enough, eh?" He smiled.

Pierre crawled over to the small hole in front of the tiny fireplace. He embraced his son and then peered down into the hole. The opening was barely big enough for a man to fit through. He looked curiously at his boy. "What must I do?"

"It is simple, Papa. Just go down feet first. It is only a three-foot shaft down to the tunnel. We dug out a larger room below." He grinned. "It is not really a room, but it is big enough for you be able to bend over and get down onto your belly. Then all you must do is crawl toward the moonlight. It is about twenty-five feet. Take your time and do not worry. We will be right behind you."

"There are men waiting at the other end?"

"Yes, Papa. You have friends there waiting for you. Now … enough of the talk. Let's go!"

Francois and little Pierre helped the sick man lower himself into the tiny hole. They held on to

Pierre's hands for a moment and then released him into the tunnel below. Pierre scraped against the coarse, rocky sides of the vertical shaft and landed in the bottom of the tunnel with a jarring thud.

He knelt down for a moment to compose himself and get his bearings. He quickly located the shaft that led to the shack. He bent forward and lay down on his belly. Once he was pointed toward the exit he did not waste any time. Pierre crawled with reckless abandon toward the dull blue glow of moonlight at the far end of the tunnel.

It was a long, painful, energy-sapping endeavor. When at long last he reached the end, a set of strong hands pulled him out of the shaft. The invisible assistant steadied Pierre and helped him stand upright. His legs were weak and trembling from the sudden exercise involved in crawling such a long distance. Pierre looked into the man's face and recognized Lieutenant Oscar Hamelin of the militia.

"Oscar!" He hugged his friend.

"It is good to see you, Pierre."

"You cannot imagine how good it is to see you, Oscar."

"What about me?" inquired another voice from the darkness. It was Captain Bousseron.

"Francois! You are here as well!" hissed Pierre.

"There was no way that I was going to miss seeing you off this night," retorted the captain. "We have worked much too hard for this. Our men needed a victory after the humiliation of our shameful surrender." The captain hugged Pierre.

Francois Turpin's head soon poked out of the end of the shaft. "Give a fellow a hand!" he whispered.

The men grabbed his arms and helped him out of the hole.

"The boy is right behind me," declared Turpin.

Moments later little Pierre crawled out of the hole and then stood proudly beside his father.

The captain declared, "We have no time to waste." He moved closer to Pierre. "You need to get moving right now. We have the canoe ready. You will launch immediately. Drift south until you reach the mouth of the Embarrass River, then turn and head upstream. Go to Indian Creek and paddle two miles west. There is an old cabin on a small hill near the creek. You can hide out at that location until you feel a little better. But you need to move on to Kaskaskia as soon as possible."

"I understand the plan, Francois. It is a good one. But I am very weak. I do not know if I have the muscle or strength to paddle against a current, even the minor current of the Embarrass River. Will someone go with me? Francois Turpin, perhaps?"

A deep voice muttered from the darkness in the far corner of the shack, "What good will that city boy do you in the backwoods?"

Pierre recognized that gruff voice, even though it was one that he had not heard in many months. His lips broke into a broad smile when the face of his good friend, Charles Rimbault, appeared in the moonlight. Charles was a boatsman and voyageur who lived on the rivers of the Illinois Country. He had departed for New Orleans almost eight months ago and Pierre had not seen him since.

"Charles, you old skunk! Where have you been? You should have returned from New Orleans a month ago!" He shook hands with his long-absent friend. The rugged river man grabbed Pierre and hugged him with a warm embrace. Emotional tears flowed down Pierre's cheeks. Though he would never admit it, old Charles had tears of joy, as well.

Charles broke the embrace and gave Pierre an enthusiastic slap on the arm. "I got tangled up in Kaskaskia, old friend. The town is full of those strange, interesting men from Virginia. I have been there for three weeks enjoying their company and their rum and relieving them of what little money they carried. It seems that none of them have any skill at cards or dice." He winked. "I only returned this very evening. Captain Bousseron informed me of your situation and the mission … so here I am. Fresh as a daisy. Are you ready?"

"You are going with me?" Pierre asked in disbelief.

"Nothing could keep me from it."

Pierre smiled. "Then I am ready."

He turned and faced his son. Little Pierre was crying. The proud father knelt beside the boy and wrapped his arms around him in a huge bear hug. "I am so very proud of you, son. And I am grateful for what you have done. I know that you have worked so very hard to set me free."

The boy wiped his tears. "Just come home as soon as you can, Papa, and bring the Virginians with you. We have a fort and a town to take back. We will be waiting for you."

He hugged his boy again.

"We must go, Pierre," urged Charles Rimbault.

Pierre released his son from his embrace. His friends helped him walk to the edge of the water and climb clumsily into the canoe. Charles insisted that he lie down in the bottom in the front of the boat and cover up with the blankets that awaited him there. The river adventurer took up a paddle and seated himself in the rear steering position.

"Good luck, and Godspeed," whispered the captain.

The captain and Francois Turpin both waded thigh-deep into the water and gave the heavy, cargo-laden canoe a vigorous shove out into the current of the Wabash River. They watched with pride as the canoe that carried their liberated compatriot disappeared silently into the winter darkness.

Part III

The Battle for Vincennes

CHAPTER TWELVE
HAMILTON'S REVENGE

Young Pierre made his way toward home after his father made his escape into the darkness of the December night. It took a long time for him to creep through the dark forests on the outskirts of Vincennes. It was only a couple of hours before dawn when he tumbled onto his soft, warm mattress beside his two little brothers.

The noise of life in the Grimard house awakened Pierre some time during the early morning. His brothers were up and running noisily throughout their small house. There was the crisp crackling of the warm fire inside the fireplace.

Pierre smelled food cooking … smoked pork and fresh bread. His mother was, no doubt, preparing a huge feast for their family Christmas celebration. And what a celebration it would be!

There were no presents to exchange this year, but Pierre did not care. He received the very best present of all when he saw his father drift downriver in that canoe. His father was free! And he had the wonderful satisfaction of knowing that he had helped him escape execution at the hands of the British.

There was joy inside the Grimard house this Christmas. The members of the frontier family were very happy. It was going to be a great day.

Suddenly there came a loud banging on the door of the house. An angry voice called from outside, "Open this door, by order of His Majesty's governor! We are here to search this house!" The banging resumed.

Pierre darted from behind the privacy curtain. He clumsily donned his breeches and tucked in his shirt. His mother's eyes met his. She was seated in her rocking chair near the fire. She was obviously terrified. Pierre moved toward the door.

His mother hissed, "Do not open it, Pierre!"

"Mama, they will knock it down if I do not open it." He frowned, and then whispered, "They are looking for Papa. You must act surprised when they tell you he is gone. You have to pretend like you don't know anything."

She nodded grimly.

Again, the voice called from the other side of the door, "Open up now, or we will be forced to break this door!"

Pierre screeched angrily, "I'm coming! Give me a moment!"

He took a deep breath and then walked to the door. He released the latch and began to open it slowly. The door flew open in his face with a tremendous force, knocking him to the floor. The boy's head hit the hard floor with a loud thud.

Genevieve screamed, "There is no need for your violence!"

"What took you so long?" boomed Major Jehu Hay, the commander of the British soldiers.

Pierre stood and rubbed the back of his throbbing head. He responded, "We were scared to open the door. We are not accustomed to fists banging on our house and soldiers shouting at us in the early morning."

"What is the meaning of this intrusion?" demanded Genevieve. "It is enough that we must endure your injustice later today when you steal the life of my husband at the end of your horrid rope!"

Major Hay grinned angrily. "As if you didn't already know …"

Genevieve's face took on a very confused look. She turned and stared at little Pierre, who pretended to be equally confused. Pierre smiled in his heart. His mother was doing a great job of pretending.

"I assure you that I have no idea what you are talking about, Major."

"Your husband has escaped!" yelled the British officer. "And with the aid of people in this town. We discovered a tunnel below his guardhouse that led to an old building near the river. It seems clear that he did not dig his own way out. There is a conspiracy at work here, Madam, and we intend to get to the bottom of it!"

Genevieve Grimard stared at the man, her eyes wide with feigned surprise. She exclaimed, "My husband has escaped?"

The Redcoat officer stared angrily at her.

She yelled again, this time in celebration, "My husband has escaped! Hallelujah! My Pierre has gone free!"

She began to skip around the room. She grabbed Pierre and began spinning him around and dancing a lively jig. Both of them laughed and cheered. Soon Jean-Baptiste and Charles joined them in a grand family celebration. It was a parade of happiness inside the tiny Grimard home.

"Enough!" shouted the officer. He turned to his men. "Search the house. Look for any sign of the fugitive."

"Surely you do not think he is here!" Genevieve protested.

"No, I am almost certain that he is not here in this house. But we must make absolutely sure, and we must search for evidence of any crime against the Crown." He glanced at one of his soldiers. "Search the house. Check everything."

"Right away, sir!" The soldier turned toward the other Redcoats. "You heard him, men! Tear this place apart!"

Two of the soldiers used their muskets to prod the members of the family through the door and into the cold outdoors. They did not even allow them the opportunity to grab a coat or blanket. Genevieve cried in protest as she clung to her children and tried to keep them warm in the winter cold. Pierre stood defiantly, arms crossed, and stared at the soldiers with a piercing glare of hate.

The squad of soldiers inside spent the next half-hour dismantling the Grimard house. They turned over cabinets and shelves. They ran their sharp bayonets through every mattress and every piece of clothing. They dumped food into the floor, including several large sacks of flour. When they were done, the house was in shambles. A thin coating of white flour covered everything inside the home.

A British sergeant reported, "The house is clear sir. No sign of the criminal Grimard."

"Very well, Sergeant. Escort the children back inside, but the woman is coming with us."

"You're not taking my mother anywhere!" screeched Pierre. He ran toward the pair of soldiers who were dragging Genevieve toward the gate. Just as he reached out and grabbed one of the men by the arm he heard and felt a loud pop in the back of his head.

And then there was nothing. The entire world turned black …

Pierre awakened several hours later. He was very disoriented. Though his surroundings looked familiar, he didn't know where he was.

He heard his little brother, Charles, proclaim, "Mama! Come quickly! Pierre is awake!"

Pierre's head was throbbing. He reached up and felt a bandage across his forehead. He reached around the back of his head and felt a hard knot.

His mother pulled a chair beside the bed and sat down. Though she was smiling, her face showed her concern. She was worried about her son.

She whispered, "How are you feeling, Pierre?"

"I'm all right, Mama. My head hurts a little."

"One of those horrible soldiers hit you in the back of the head with his musket. I could not do anything to help you. They dragged me off to the fort. Mr. and Mrs. Turpin brought you to their home and took care for you. That is where we are now."

Pierre was confused. "Why aren't we at our house?"

"Oh, son, those soldiers made a horrible mess at our place. It will take days to put everything back in order. We will have to get new mattresses and curtains. Our cabinets will have to be rebuilt. There is much damage. But do not worry, our friends and neighbors are helping us."

Pierre saw something strange about his mother's face. Her hair hung low over her right eye. It was odd … she never wore her hair like that. And it appeared that her eye was swollen.

"Mama, what is wrong with your eye?" demanded Pierre.

"Oh, nothing, dear. I'm quite all right." She began to get up from her chair but her son grabbed her wrist.

"Mama, show me."

Genevieve reached up and pulled her shiny hair away from her eye. The skin of her upper cheek and her entire eyelid were swollen and purple.

"What happened to you? Who did this to you?" he demanded.

"It is none of your concern, son. Now just lay back and let me fetch you some soup."

Again she tried to rise, but Pierre refused to release his grip.

"I am making it my concern, Mama. Now tell me … who did this to you?" His voice was harsh. He had never spoken to his mother in such a tone.

She stared in shame at the floor. Tears welled in both eyes and flowed down her cheeks. She still did not answer.

A deep voice responded from the far side of the room. "Henry Hamilton did that, Pierre." It was the voice of Francois Turpin. He was standing in front of the fireplace and puffing on his pipe. "He questioned your mother in the fort. When he didn't get the answers that he was looking for he struck her." Francois spit into the fireplace in disgust.

Pierre shifted his gaze from the angry man to his mother. "Is that true, Mama?"

Genevieve Grimard merely nodded. She did not speak.

Pierre growled under his breath. He felt rage brewing from deep inside his heart. His hands trembled and ached. He released the grip on his mother's arm. She quickly stood and walked over to the wash pan. She busied herself by washing dishes with Mrs. Turpin. Pierre could hear her weeping.

Mr. Turpin walked toward the bed. "Don't worry about your mother, Pierre. She is a fine, strong woman." He sat down in the chair that Genevieve had placed beside the bed. Gaspard joined him at the wounded boy's bedside. The boy brought Pierre a cup of hot tea with honey. He punched his best friend affectionately in the shoulder and then sat down on the foot of the bed.

Francois continued, "Pierre, I saw that mother of yours endure much worse things on our journey up the Mississippi River from New Orleans." He paused and chuckled. "Did you know that your father and mother once saved my life?"

Mrs. Turpin sighed and exclaimed, "Not that story again!" She grinned. Gaspard laughed. Genevieve continued drying dishes in silence.

"Truly, Mr. Turpin? They saved your life?"

"Oh, yes. We were still in the Louisiana Territory, not even two weeks out of New Orleans, when I went out on a hunting expedition with your papa. I stepped in a hole full of deadly snakes. Four of them bit me through my moccasin. I was dead, for sure. But your father rescued me from the woods. He tied a belt around my thigh and then cut my leg open and drained the poison. He had men carry me in a litter back to the boats. Then your sweet mother nursed me back to health and cared for me for several weeks during the journey. She fed me and gave me water with a spoon when I was unable to drink. I surely would have died had it not been for your parents."

"She really did that?" asked Pierre in disbelief.

"Indeed she did! And on top of that every man on that journey was scared to death of her! She ran our camp like a Hessian general. Those eighty boatsmen took off running every time they saw her coming. Why, even old Charles Rimbault, the famous river explorer of Vincennes, was scared of Genevieve Grimard!"

Everyone in the house laughed. Even Genevieve could not help giggling. Pierre was glad to hear joy in his mother's voice again.

Francois paused and leaned toward Pierre. "So, don't go getting all worked up over a black eye. Your mama is stronger than any punch thrown by Henry Hamilton."

He sat back in the chair, sucked in a long draw from his pipe, and then exhaled the gray-blue smoke.

"Anyhow, your mama is a legend in Vincennes now. She stood up to Henry Hamilton and made him so angry that he struck her. That swollen eye is her badge of courage."

Pierre was surprised. He had never heard the snakebite story. He liked the idea of his mother saving a man's life. He always knew that his father was a brave, strong man. But he was beginning to realize that his mother was a steady, strong person, as well. He was proud of his mama … but he still despised Henry Hamilton.

Gaspard exclaimed, "Tell him about how Mama fell out of a tornado and became your wife!"

Pierre's eyes grew wide with surprise.

Francois chuckled and tugged on his son's foot. "That, my boy, is a very long story. We will save it for another day. Now, let's get Pierre up and out of this bed and get a little hot soup into his belly."

In the weeks that followed, life under the British became exceedingly difficult. Governor Hamilton was livid when he discovered that Pierre Grimard has escaped from his guardhouse. He became even more frustrated when he could not locate any evidence of the conspiracy to set the prisoner free. His anger quickly reached a boiling point.

The governor decided to take out his frustrations on the people of the town. He imposed harsh rules and curfews upon the citizens. He broke down doors in the middle of the night and carried men off to jail. He ordered his troops to take food and supplies from the townsfolk. He did everything that he could think of to make the lives of the French people in Vincennes as difficult as possible.

The weather made life in the Illinois Country even more miserable. Though the winter had not yet turned frigid, the country was shrouded in rain and cold. Soaking rains fell almost daily. The rivers and streams were swollen and overflowing. The Wabash River flooded thousands of acres of bottomland at the southern end of the village. The streets of the town became muddy lakes. The rains of January became even heavier in the first week of February.

The people of Vincennes continued to do what they had always done. They struggled to survive.

They fought against the weather, hunger, and disease. They endured the oppression off the British. And they counted the days until the Americans under Colonel George Rogers Clark would return and, once again, bring liberty and freedom to their tiny frontier village.

CHAPTER THIRTEEN
VISITORS IN THE NIGHT

February 5, 1779

Pierre's feet were soaking wet and frozen. He had run off into the pitch black of night to find Mrs. Turpin and bring her back to the Grimard home. On the way he stumbled into a huge puddle of water and thoroughly soaked his buckskin moccasins.

Pierre longed to warm his feet beside the fire, but that would have to wait. He had to take care of his younger brothers and keep them behind the curtain where the boys slept. Their mother needed her privacy. She was in the middle of giving birth.

Beyond the curtain, Genevieve wailed from the pain of childbirth. Jean-Baptiste and Charles stared at their big brother in wide-eyed fear. Gaspard Turpin, who had accompanied his mother to the Grimard home, seemed concerned, as well.

"It's been going on for a long time," Gaspard whispered. "We should have heard the baby cry before now."

"Everything is all right," Pierre assured the other boys quietly. "Mama will be all better once her baby is out."

He desperately wanted to believe his own words. At the same time, his heart ached with worry for his mother.

Soon they heard Josephine Turpin's commanding voice from the other side of the curtain. "All right, little mama, we're almost done. Now, just one more push, Genevieve! This is it! One more push! Do it now! Push, woman, push!"

They heard Genevieve groan. She screamed loudly, and then suddenly became very quiet.

"It is a girl!" Josephine shrieked. "It is a perfect little girl!"

Pierre looked excitedly at his little brothers. "Did you hear that, boys? We have a baby sister!"

"Aww …" complained Charles. "I wanted a brother." He crossed his arms in disgust.

The other boys giggled quietly.

Soon they heard the dull whack of Mrs. Turpin's hand hitting the child's bottom. The baby coughed and sputtered for a moment and then emitted a high-pitched, powerful, piercing cry. Both Genevieve and Josephine joined in with their own cries of celebration and joy.

"You did a wonderful job!" declared Josephine. "You should be very pleased with yourself."

"I want to see!" declared little Charles. Pierre tried to hold him back, but he bolted from his big brother's grip and ran to the curtain to peek through into the room where his mother lay. The other boys shrugged and joined him. The four curious boys watched through the crack in the curtains and listened.

"I simply cannot believe that I finally have a baby girl," Genevieve proclaimed through tears of joy. "I have wanted a little girl of my own for so very long." She gently kissed the newborn's eyes and nose and then held her tiny, pink cheek up against her own.

Josephine glanced toward the privacy curtains that were drawn shut across the far end of the room. Several glowing eyes stared in her direction through the narrow crack between the two drapes. She smiled.

"All right, boys. You can come out now. Come and meet your new sister. Gaspard, you can come out, as well. Come and greet the newest member of the Grimard household!"

The Grimard boys darted instantly from behind the curtain, scampered across the room, and surrounded their mother. She held the baby out for them to examine. Their faces beamed with wonder and joy. Gaspard, Josephine's son, stood behind them and looked at the baby in silent curiosity.

"Oh, Mama, she is so pretty!" declared Jean-Baptiste.

The rambunctious Charles, barely three years old and still something of a baby himself, didn't have anything to say. He simply climbed up onto the bed beside his mother and, without invitation, planted a firm kiss on the baby girl's forehead. Genevieve's heart leapt.

"I think she looks like Papa," declared Pierre. "Look at her long, wavy hair. And she has Papa's eyes!"

Genevieve held the little girl up and examined her closely. "I do think you are right, Pierre. And if she looks like your papa then she must also look like you, because you are his perfect image." She lay the baby back on her chest and reached out to cup her hand against her oldest son's cheek. Little Pierre turned his head and kissed his mother's hand with tender affection.

"Whatever shall you call her?" asked Josephine. "Pierre is not here to help you choose the name."

"We already selected names several months ago. If it were a boy he was to be called Nicolas."

"Well, you will just have to save that name for the next baby, perhaps. But what name for a girl?"

Genevieve smiled. "Pierre insisted that a girl be named with the most beautiful name that he has ever heard or spoken from his lips." She paused.

"And?" Josephine asked impatiently. "Do not keep us in suspense. What is this most beautiful name?"

"Why, it is Genevieve, of course!"

Both women and the room full of little boys giggled with joy.

February 23, 1779

The last whispers of sunlight had disappeared from the tiny window. The world outside the Grimard home was shrouded in the dark purples and grays of night. Genevieve wiped sweat from her brow in desperation. Her children had become quite unruly. The tired woman was almost at her wit's end. She wanted her children to go to bed so that she might have some peace.

Three weeks had passed since giving birth to baby Genevieve. The infant was suffering terribly from belly aches. She cried and fussed almost without ceasing. The rambunctious Grimard boys were of no help whatsoever. It was time for bed, yet all the lads wanted to do was pretend to shoot muskets and play war, fall out in the floor and "play dead," and cause an overall din of madness and confusion inside the house.

Genevieve screeched in weary anger, "Jean-Baptiste, I want you and Charles to stop all of that screaming and unnecessary noise and get into bed! Right now! I am tired of your constant wrestling and rough play inside my house. Daylight will come early tomorrow, and both of you will have many chores to do. Now get behind that curtain right now and crawl beneath those covers!"

"Yes, Mama," responded the older boy as he darted obediently toward his pallet in the corner. Charles followed, as well, though he continued to poke and trip his older brother on the way to their destination.

Genevieve scolded the younger boy, "Charles! Stop it, immediately! Do not make me come in there and put you in that bed!"

The lad complied, though he continued to sport a mischievous grin as he disappeared behind the curtain. Genevieve covered her mouth to keep from laughing at the unruly boy.

Genevieve saw the larger hand of her ever-responsible oldest son, Pierre, as he reached up to pull the curtain closed. The exhausted mother breathed a prayer of thanksgiving and then sat down in her rocking chair to attempt to nurse her fussy baby. She relaxed for the briefest of moments and closed her eyes. She jumped in fear when she heard a subtle, hollow knock at the front door.

She froze in fear. Who could it possibly be? No one ventured out after dark. Governor Hamilton had declared a sundown curfew on the town since Christmas Day. Anyone caught moving around after dark was treated as an enemy spy.

She heard a deep, hollow cough from beyond the door.

Little Pierre had heard the knock, as well. He darted from behind the bedroom curtain, clad in only a long indigo shirt and stocking feet. He grabbed the pistol that hung on a rack beside the fireplace, then cast a glance at his mother. Her eyes met her son's as he stepped forward and placed his hand on the latch. She nodded to him.

Pierre placed his face close to the rough planks of the door and whispered, "Who is there?"

A familiar voice emanated from beyond the door, "It is I! The man of this house!"

"Papa!" squealed little Pierre.

He flung open the door and froze in horror at the sight of the filthy, hairy, smelly man who lurked in the shadows of their covered porch. Genevieve appeared instantly at her son's side. She, too, froze in utter disbelief.

Pierre coughed deeply and then spoke hoarsely, "Well … must I stand here in the frigid night, or might I come inside and visit with my family for a while?" He grinned, revealing a gleaming row of pearly teeth behind the whiskers and grime.

Genevieve, still clutching her infant daughter, tumbled into Pierre's arms. She wept. Young Pierre quickly closed the door behind his father and then jumped and shouted in celebration.

The other children, curious as to the identity of their nighttime visitor, quickly spilled from behind the privacy curtain. When they saw their mother in the visitor's arms they realized that it could only be their father. They descended with childlike enthusiasm upon their long-absent papa. Pierre hugged and kissed each one of them.

Genevieve held the baby in front of her husband. "Pierre Grimard, I would like for you to meet your daughter, Genevieve." She smiled. The baby wailed from hunger.

Tears began to streak Pierre's filthy cheeks. He turned his head to the side and coughed. He looked lovingly at the baby and then into the eyes of his wife. "It is a girl?" he asked in disbelief.

"Yes, my love. We finally have a baby girl in the family."

He examined the child. "Is she well? Does she have all of her fingers and toes?"

Genevieve giggled. "She is perfect!"

Pierre took the infant in his arms. She cried even louder. He held the little girl's face close to his and kissed her gently on her tiny, pink nose. He cried from absolute joy.

Genevieve joined in his weeping, and then babbled through her tears, "I do not understand, Pierre. From whence did you come? Why are you here? You know how dangerous it is for you to be in Vincennes!"

Pierre, holding the baby in the crook of his right arm, pulled his wife closer with his left.

"I am not alone, my love. I have come back with the army of the Long Knives."

She pushed back from his chest and stared wide-eyed. "The Americans are here?" she hissed.

"Yes. Colonel Clark's army is on the outskirts of the village. They will soon invade the town and launch their attack on the fort. I came under orders to deliver a message to Captain Bousseron so that he might instruct the local families to remain concealed inside their homes."

Genevieve lay her head against Pierre's shoulder. "How long will you stay?"

"I am released until dawn tomorrow, when I must report back to the Colonel and join in the fighting. So tonight, I am allowed to stay here in my own home."

He smiled warmly. "But the other answer to your question is, 'forever.' I am never leaving Vincennes or you or my children again."

Genevieve released herself from his embrace and marched very deliberately toward her rocking chair. She wiped her tears as she went. She declared, "Well, if that is the case, you are going to have to do a bit of cleaning up if you plan to sleep in my clean house tonight." She plopped down into the chair with an air of authority. "Bring me my hungry daughter, please."

Pierre complied, smiling from ear to ear. His eyes twinkled with delight.

"Junior!" she barked.

"Yes, Mama?"

"Hang a pot of water over the fire. Your papa must do some bathing. Once I am finished with Genevieve I will shave his shaggy face and dispose of those horrible, prickly whiskers."

"Yes, Mama."

"And fetch your father some fresh clothes. We are going to have to burn these filthy rags he is wearing."

"All right, Mama," responded Pierre as he darted to the shelf to find a clean shirt and breeches for his father.

"Pierre, are you hungry?"

Once again Pierre coughed deeply. There was a hollow, resonating gurgle in his throat and lungs. "I ate some bread and milk at Bousseron's store just a little while ago. But I am still famished. We have been starving for over a week. We ran out of food during the trek."

"I suspected as much. You look like a malnourished ghost. There is some venison stew still in the warming pot. Help yourself to it and the bread."

Pierre coughed deeply.

Genevieve shook her head. "That cough sounds terrible. I will coat you down with salve and mint after you are clean."

"Yes, Madame General," replied Pierre sarcastically as he lifted his right hand for a crisp salute. He leaned down and kissed his wife on the forehead. "It is so very good to be home."

Genevieve grinned with delight.

Pierre and his brothers were too excited to sleep. They asked their father dozens of questions. He told them the amazing story of how the starving army of Virginians, the Long Knives under Colonel George Rogers Clark, had waded and swam through over a hundred miles of cold water to reach Vincennes. Pierre tried to imagine what it must have been like to take part in such a heroic journey. How he wished he had been there!

His father was in the middle of telling them a most amazing story. He told about two nights previous when his clothing had frozen to his body during the night. He was just getting to the climax of his story when gunfire erupted in the town.

Genevieve flinched and jerked her hand at the sudden and nearby blast of the rifles. Her razor nicked Pierre's chin, drawing blood. There were over a dozen thunderous shots in quick succession.

"I am so sorry, husband!" She reached for the small cloth that floated in the steaming hot shave water.

Pierre simply grinned and plugged the cut with his thumb. He was about to respond to her apology, but was interrupted by a chorus of screeches and howls in the night. Moments later it sounded as if hundreds of savage voices had joined in the horrible, fearful din. At least two dozen howling, screaming men ran past the front gate of the Grimard house.

Genevieve's lip quivered. It appeared that she was on the verge of tears. "Is it the Indians? Are they attacking our village?"

Pierre placed a reassuring hand on her arm. "No, my darling. Those are our friends from Virginia and the brave Frenchmen from the villages to the west. The attack has commenced."

Soon more shots thundered from throughout the village, all aimed at the walls of Fort Sackville.

CHAPTER FOURTEEN
CANNON BALLS AND MUSKET BALLS

Pierre could barely sleep. He was too excited. Besides, the entire world outside was so loud, how could anyone sleep? Beyond the walls of his home gunfire raged as the Virginians and Frenchmen poured their musket and rifle fire into the walls of the fort. He tried to envision how frightened those British soldiers concealed within the fort must be.

But what was most exciting was the fact that his father was home! He could only imagine the adventures that he and his band of spies would have after the sunrise. They would, most definitely, have to perform missions and tasks to support the fighting. The American army would need help to win back the fort for the British.

As Pierre dozed he dreamed about the great battle. The sounds of the real muskets outside the house made it the most vivid dream he had ever experienced. There was even the great boom of artillery …

A sudden explosion and the crack of shattering wood ripped little Pierre from his slumber. He jumped up from his mattress and ran past the curtain to where his parents slept.

"Papa, was that thunder?"

"No, son. The British are firing their cannons. We have to move someplace safe. Get dressed as quickly as you can and then help your mother to get your brothers ready."

"Yes, Papa."

Another explosion jarred their home. This time dust fell from the rafters and shingles overhead.

Genevieve inquired frantically as she tied the cords of her skirt around her waist, "Where will we go? To the church?"

Her husband shook his head. "It is not safe there, either. The church is closer to the fort and the fighting. We must move east, out of the line of fire from their towers. Bousseron's store is far enough in that direction. Quickly, let us get the children dressed and go there. Perhaps he will give us shelter. But we need to make sure everyone is dressed warmly. We may be outside for quite a while."

Pierre shouted at his sons behind their curtain, "Boys, wear your coats and caps! Dress as if you were going on a hunting trip with me."

The boys responded, "Yes, Papa!"

Young Pierre sat on his feather-stuffed mattress as he slipped his fur-lined moccasins onto his feet. Suddenly the deafening sound of shattering wood filled the entire house. The wall to his left seemed to disappear as it tumbled inward. He heard his mother scream. He heard his father cry out in pain. His little brothers screamed and cried, as well.

A British cannon ball decimated the Grimard home. Pierre's nostrils filled with dust as the walls of the house collapsed around him. He and his brothers were, miraculously, in the one corner of the house that was not completely destroyed.

Pierre reached out through the smoke and haze and felt for his brothers.

"Jean! Charles! Are you all right?"

Jean-Baptiste responded, "I am fine."

Charles whimpered, "My head hurts."

"Come toward my voice," Pierre commanded them.

Seconds later his little brothers emerged from beneath two large boards that were leaning against a nearby shelf. The boards appeared to be pieces of the roof that had fallen into the collapsed house. Pierre grabbed each of the boys by the arm.

"Come with me. We have to find a way out of here. Do not let go of one another."

Pierre turned and made his way toward an open spot in the rubble of the house. There was fire everywhere. He somehow managed to weave his way through the debris. His brothers followed close behind him. They soon emerged into the cold air and darkness outside.

The yard was bathed in an eerie orange-yellow light from several small fires. Pierre scanned the area around him. It appeared that there were at least three other houses or shops nearby that were on fire.

Francois and Josephine Turpin appeared out of the darkness, running from the direction of their home. "Pierre! Boys! Are you injured?"

Pierre helped his brothers climb over a pile of loose, smoking boards. "We are all right, Mr. Turpin. Charles was hit in the head, but I think he will be fine."

"Pierre, you're bleeding!" exclaimed Josephine, pointing to his right leg.

Pierre looked down and saw blood flowing from a cut just above his knee. He knelt down and examined the wound. "It's nothing, Mrs. Turpin … just a scratch."

"Where are your parents?" asked Francois.

Pierre shook his head and coughed. The smoke was beginning to irritate his throat and lungs. "I have not seen them. They must be beneath the house."

Francois began to shout, "Help! Help us! The Grimards are buried! Help!"

"You boys come over here with me," urged Josephine. "We must keep you warm."

She almost dragged Jean-Baptiste and Charles across the street, where she made them sit on a neighbor's porch. She squatted down between them and, like a mother hen, draped the blanket that was wrapped around her shoulders across both boys to help keep them warm. She shouted, "Pierre, come keep warm with us!"

Pierre, standing in the debris that was once his home, yelled back, "I have to find Mama and Papa!" He joined Francois and a growing group of other men who were pulling boards and stones from the smoldering pile.

The gunfire near the fort continued, but the cannon fire had stopped. For a while, at least, Pierre forgot about the battle. He paid no attention to the shooting. All he could think about was his family.

Several minutes later one of the men exclaimed, "They are over here! I have found them!"

Pierre and the other searchers swarmed to the spot. As Pierre got closer to the rescue team he could hear baby Genevieve crying. The infant's angry wail made him smile. His baby sister had survived! Then he heard one of the men shout in celebration, "They are all alive!"

A gigantic cheer filled the night. Within minutes the men had safely removed Pierre's mother and baby sister from the wreckage. He ran to them. His mother, clutching her baby in her arms, smiled when she saw her oldest son.

She cried out, "Pierre! Are my boys safe?"

"We are all safe, Mother. Mrs. Turpin has Jean and Charles across the street." He examined his mother. She did not appear to have any injuries. "How is Papa?"

She shook her head. "I do not know. I never heard him speak, even when we were trapped next to one another beneath the timbers. Please check on him, Pierre!"

The boy nodded. He turned and climbed up on top of the pile to get closer to the men who were digging his father out. He shouted, "Mr. Turpin! Is my father all right?"

Francois answered from the darkness, "He is alive, Pierre, but unconscious. I believe he was hit in the head. We almost have him free. We will know more in a moment."

It took several more minutes to extract his father from the remnants of his home. When the men finally pulled him out he was quite a mess. They carried him from the debris pile and laid him on the porch of a nearby house. Genevieve left her baby with Josephine and quickly joined the rescuers.

Pierre had a large chunk of wood embedded in his back. There was also a huge knot and bleeding cut on the back of his head. He remained unconscious, but his breathing was strong and steady, despite the gurgle of fluid deep in his lungs.

Francois frowned. "This sickness in his chest is not going to help things one bit."

Little Pierre wasn't worried about that. He was too busy examining his father's wounds. "How did that piece of wood get in his back?"

"Shrapnel from the cannon blast," Francois surmised. "When the cannon ball exploded inside your home it shattered some of the timbers into small fragments. This one stuck in your papa's back, almost like a huge splinter."

"Can you get it out?" wailed Genevieve.

"Most definitely. But that is the least of our worries. I am more concerned about the injury to his head. Right now we need to get him some place safe … away from the cannons and the fighting," declared Francois Turpin. "But where can we take him?"

"How about the mill?" suggested Pierre. "It is a strong building made of stone and far from the fort."

"That's an excellent idea, Pierre!"

Francois stood and cupped his hands to his mouth. "Take all of the injured people to the grain mill! Anyone who needs shelter … go to the mill! We will set up a hospital there!"

Word began to spread instantly about the aid station that was to be established at the mill. People began walking in that direction.

Francois knelt down beside the injured Pierre. He brushed back the hair from the man's face and whispered, "Hang in there, old friend. We will take good care of you. I promise."

Three men appeared with a large wool blanket. They unfolded the blanket flat on the ground and then carefully lifted Pierre and placed him in the center of it. Francois joined the three men, each one of them grabbing a corner of the blanket. They lifted the makeshift stretcher off of the ground and began running down the street toward the mill.

Eight Hours Later

The Morning of February 24, 1779

"No, Gaspard. Like this … tuck in the little flap right here." Pierre knelt down beside his friend and demonstrated once more the fine art of rolling a paper cartridge.

Just outside the building where they worked the Americans and the French militia continued their assault upon the fort. The battle was less than fifty yards away. The sun had been up for about a half-hour. Pierre noticed that the amount of shooting around the fort had increased dramatically in the early morning daylight.

The young spies inside Bousseron's store were lucky compared to the soldiers who were outside in the freezing cold. In addition to the warm fire, Captain Bousseron even provided the boys with mugs full of warm milk and hot tea. Overall, it was not bad duty.

Pierre and his friends were assigned to the cartridge-rolling crew. Several of the older teen-age boys of Vincennes were working at the fireplace, melting lead in ladles and pouring the molten metal into bullet molds. Together the two teams provided much-needed ammunition for the men engaged in the battle for Fort Sackville.

The boys worked feverishly to keep their little assembly line moving. These individual loads of ammunition for the army muskets were critical for the success of the American and French soldiers. Each cartridge had to be constructed properly and hold exactly the right amount of gunpowder. The American forces were counting on these boys to do the job right.

It had been a long night. After making sure his family was safely inside the protection of the mill, Pierre was the first one to make his way to Captain Bousseron's store. The captain initially put him to work as a runner. The other boys of the young spy network began to trickle in throughout the night to offer their services to the militia.

At first the captain scolded the boys for being out in the streets while a battle was raging. Then, when he was finished with his lecture about safety and how a "battle was no place for boys," he immediately put them to work pouring lead and rolling cartridges.

Pierre and Gaspard rolled dozens of hollow paper tubes, Jean-Luc carefully measured gunpowder and filled the tubes, and lastly Adrien added the lead ball and tied the ends with thread. When completed, each rolled cartridge was ready for immediate use in the battle. Men in need of ammunition came in and out of the store on a regular basis. Each time they entered the building they grabbed every cartridge that the boys had finished and then ran back out the door.

Pierre inquired as they continued their monotonous work, "Has anyone heard from Quentin?"

The boys all cut their eyes at one another and shook their heads grimly.

"I hope that he is all right," declared Adrien. "I heard that his house was hit by the cannon, too."

"I heard the captain say that no one died from the cannon fire," added Jean-Luc. "Perhaps he is helping his family at the mill."

Pierre shook his head. "I took my family some food only a short while ago. His family was not there."

"Then maybe they're at the church," suggested Gaspard.

"Could be," responded Pierre. "But there's no way for us to find out. I think we're stuck here for a while."

"Yeah," agreed Jean-Luc. "I don't expect that anyone will be volunteering to take our places any time soon." The other boys groaned in agreement.

Captain Bousseron's voice boomed from the front of the room. "Pierre Grimard! Come over here!"

Pierre jumped to his feet and ran to his captain. The militia commander stood beside a large barrel next to the front door. He held four large leather bags in his hands. There were eight powder horns stacked on top of the barrel.

The captain nodded at Pierre. "Son, how is your family?"

"They're fine, sir. I took breakfast to them a short while ago. Papa was still sleeping when I left them at the mill. They got that piece of wood out of his back and bandaged the knot on his head. He's tough. He will be just fine. Mama was taking care of the little ones."

"Good. That is truly good to hear. You father is a good man … one of my best soldiers." He paused and took a deep breath. "Pierre, you boys are doing a fine job with the cartridges, but we cannot seem to keep up with the needs of the soldiers. There are simply too many of them. We need to adjust our strategy."

"What do you need me to do, sir?"

Captain Bousseron smiled and patted Pierre on the shoulder. "Always ready to volunteer, eh, Pierre?"

"Definitely, sir!"

Bousseron nodded his head toward Pierre's friends. "The other boys are doing fine constructing the cartridges. I need you for another mission. I want you to take bags of lead balls and horns of powder out to the men on the line. But you must be careful! You need to stay low and keep behind the barricades that our men have built. Do not expose yourself to any enemy fire, do you understand?"

Pierre nodded. "I can do that."

"Good." Captain Bousseron pointed to the west. "Make your first run over toward the church and then work your way down the line. When you need more supplies, come back here and stock up. Leave full powder horns with the men who need them. Bring the empty powder horns back here to be refilled."

"Yes, sir. While I'm over that way I will check and see if Quentin is at the church. There is too much ground for me to cover alone. I could use the help."

The captain nodded. "That is a good idea. Just keep your head down. I do not think I could ever face your father and mother again if something happened to you."

Pierre grinned. "I will be fine, Captain. You can count on me."

"I know I can, Pierre. That is why I selected you for this job. You have earned the right to take part in this battle for your home and village."

"Thank you, Captain."

"You're welcome, Private Grimard. Now get loaded up and get moving!"

Pierre's mind raced. His chest swelled with pride. The captain called him, 'Private Grimard!' He was officially in the militia! He quickly took off his hand-knit cap and draped two heavy leather bags full of lead balls over each shoulder. Next, he hung two horns of powder around his neck.

He chirped, "I'm ready, sir!"

"Good. Go out the back door. The front is too exposed to fire from the fort. I'll be here when you return."

Pierre saluted and answered, "Yes, sir!" He scampered through the store and bounded through the back door.

CHAPTER FIFTEEN
VICTORY!

Pierre was thrilled when he found his friend Quentin safe and uninjured at the church. He hauled his fellow spy back to Bousseron's store and loaded the boy down with bags full of musket and rifle balls and several powder horns.

The boys made deliveries along the front line throughout the morning. Soon their cargo began to include baskets full of snacks and food for the hungry soldiers. They also delivered canteens and buckets full of drinking water. The boys worked nonstop throughout the morning.

There had been a brief break in the fighting around mid-morning as the two forces met under the white flags of truce. Colonel George Rogers Clark attempted to coax Governor Henry Hamilton into surrendering his forces and giving up the fort. The conference ended quickly, however, and the battle soon resumed.

The elder Pierre Grimard, despite his wounded back and throbbing head, insisted on taking part in the fight. He, Francois Turpin, and Charles Rimbault joined the men on the front line a short time after the brief cease-fire. Soon they, too, were shooting at the walls of the fort.

Like everyone else, they were not firing at anything in particular. They simply shot at the fort. They could, on occasion, see movement along the tops of the walls or through the wider holes in the chinking, but it was silly to think that they could actually hit such difficult targets with their muskets. Their weapons were simply not accurate enough for such sharpshooting.

Charles Rimbault, the rough and wild river explorer, fired a few shots when they first joined the line, but he quickly became bored with shooting at logs. He decided, instead, to find a soft spot in the loose dirt and lie down until, as he stated, "There was something to shoot at that might actually bleed." Amazingly, he made a nest behind the barricade and fell sound asleep in the midst of the constant thunder of gunfire. For the next hour Pierre and Francois continued to fire their muskets at nothing in particular.

"Charles is right!" Francois finally declared in disgust. "This is a monumental waste of powder and lead!"

"It is all for a strategic purpose," answered Pierre. "At least the British are keeping their heads down. I have not heard a single shot from inside the fort since we arrived on the line. I think that is what Colonel Clark wants us to do … keep the enemy hunkered down and out of the battle." He frowned. "Because it will be bloody, indeed, if we actually have to attack and storm the walls of that fort."

Francois shuddered at the notion. "I want no part of that."

A high-pitched voice interrupted their conversation. "Do you need anything, Papa?"

Pierre spun around and saw his son, Pierre, kneeling behind him and holding a large basket covered with a white linen napkin. He also carried two large leather bags under each arm. It was a wonder that the spunky nine-year-old was able to walk at all with such a heavy load of cargo.

"Pierre! Son! What are you doing wandering among the earthworks and defenses? Do you not understand how dangerous it is up here?"

"I was careful, Papa. Anyhow, there has not been a shot from inside the fort since the parley earlier this morning." The boy grinned triumphantly at his father.

Pierre growled in disgust. "How in the world do you know about military matters? You are but a lad!" He pointed to a small depression behind a large log. "Stay low and sit down right there." His voice was harsh.

The boy complied. His grin never left his face.

"What is in the basket?" asked Charles from beneath the hat that still covered his face. Young Pierre gave the man a puzzled look. He had no idea how the supposedly sleeping Frenchman even knew that he was carrying a basket.

"Just some food for the soldiers on the line, Mr. Charles. I have been making deliveries. There is bread and jam, and a little bit of smoked, dried buffalo."

"What is in the bags?" asked Francois.

Little Pierre grinned and patted the bags on his right side. ".69 caliber Charleville musket balls on this side and .44 caliber rifle balls on the other."

Francois chuckled and shook his head. "Have you seen my son?"

"I left Gaspard with the other boys who were pouring lead and rolling cartridges. He seemed happy and content inside Bousseron's store. There is a warm fire and hot tea in there."

"Have you seen your mother recently?" asked his father as he reloaded his musket.

Little Pierre nodded. "I checked on them a short time ago. She is fine, and the children are well. They have actually returned home with Mrs. Turpin. Jean and Charles are sound asleep."

Little Pierre nodded toward Francois. "Sir, your wife said that the mill was no place for the little ones. Now that the town seems safe from the cannons, most of the women have returned to their homes and warm fires. She invited our family to share your home until ours is repaired."

Francois nodded and smiled. "She's a good woman … my Josephine."

His father smiled, as well. "That is good news, indeed. What about you, son? How are you holding up?"

"I am a bit tired, but I will be fine. I have been working hard throughout the night and morning. This is my last trip to the line for a while. I plan to go to Mr. Turpin's house as soon as I finish my rounds and all of my bags are empty. I could use a nap."

A voice soon bellowed from a Virginia officer down the line, "Maintain fire on the fort! You gentlemen can rest when the war is over!" They looked in the direction of the voice. It was clear that the man was talking directly to them.

Pierre winked at his son as he poured a touch of powder from his horn into his pan. "We need to get back to work, son. You can leave us some of that bread before you go."

Little Pierre nodded and grabbed a foot-long loaf of bread from the basket, along with a small crock of apple jam. He hesitated briefly and appeared to have something to say.

"What is the matter, son?"

"I was just wondering …"

"Wondering what?"

"I was just wondering what it is like to actually fight … you know … to shoot at the fort. All I've done is deliver stuff." He looked longingly at his father. There was a moment of awkward silence and expectation.

"Let the boy fire your musket, Pierre," encouraged Francois. "You know he deserves it. He has served as much as any other man of Vincennes throughout the night." Francois turned, aimed, and fired his weapon. A billowing cloud of white smoke swirled over the top of them.

"Francois is right," chimed Charles from beneath his hat. "Let the lad shoot a time or two. He can shoot at lumber just as well as you fellows."

Pierre pondered his friends' words for a moment and then grinned at his boy. "Put your basket down and come over here."

Little Pierre eagerly dropped his basket to the ground and crawled toward his father. He made sure to keep his head behind the protection of the logs, boards, and earth.

"I have a perfect little hole over here that you can fire through. But I do not want you to raise your head above this pile of dirt. You can just aim at the logs of the fort and then shoot … one time. All right?"

Little Pierre nodded.

"Get on your knees right here and hold the stock against your shoulder. I will help you."

Pierre stuck the barrel of the musket through the firing hole. He helped his son get into position and then knelt behind him.

"Can you see the wall?"

"Yes, Papa."

"Try to pick a large crack between the logs and aim for it."

Little Pierre nodded.

"All right, I am pulling the lock back to full cock. Now, remember … it is going to kick hard. It might hurt your shoulder." He tugged on the hammer until it locked with a hollow 'click.' "You can shoot whenever you are ready."

Little Pierre paused as he aimed at a small hole in the wall of the fort. He could almost swear that he saw movement beyond the hole. The boy was trembling with excitement and anticipation. He thought, "There must be a British soldier behind that wall!" He could scarcely breathe or even think.

Pierre yanked the trigger. The massive musket belched fire and smoke and kicked hard against his shoulder, knocking him backwards into his father's chest. He lowered the stock and rubbed his sore shoulder. The soot of the gunpowder ignition streaked and stained his face.

Charles Rimbault lifted his hat from his own face and grinned broadly. "Congratulations, Pierre. You killed a dead tree." He winked at the boy.

Francois looked at the lad and chuckled. "Well, just look at that! Little Pierre, musketeer and Patriot of the Vincennes Militia!"

Pierre smiled so big that his face ached.

Later that Afternoon

The guns around the fort were silent. Another cease-fire had been called. Pierre and the other boys among his band of spies gathered at the front of the store and watched as three men left the fort and met Colonel Clark and two of his officers in front of the Catholic Church. Captain Bousseron stood beside Pierre.

"What are they doing, Captain?" asked Quentin.

"Hopefully they are negotiating a surrender," responded Bousseron. "I certainly hope so. Taking this fort will be difficult and deadly otherwise."

"I heard my papa say that it would be very bloody if it came down to that," declared Pierre.

"Indeed, it would, son. Very bloody. Many men on both sides will die. Let us hope that these officers can come to an agreement that will spare the lives of both our men and theirs."

Captain Bousseron looked proudly at the five boys. "You lads have done excellent work today. We could not have fought this battle without you. I'm proud to have all of you serving under my command."

The lads grinned and their faces flushed red from embarrassment.

"I want you boys to go home and get some food and rest. We are all caught up on ammunition and food for now. If you do not hear any more shooting today, you may remain off-duty and at home. But report back to me first thing in the morning. Understood?"

The boys screeched, "Yes, sir!"

"Good. Now get out of here!" The captain swatted Gaspard on the behind. He laughed as the five lads jumped off of the porch and ran toward their homes.

February 25, 1779

10:00 A.M. - Near the Gates of Fort Sackville

The fighting had stopped. The battle was over. Governor Hamilton finally realized that he could not win against the Long Knives and their French allies. He accepted the terms of surrender.

Colonel Clark agreed to hold a formal surrender ceremony directly in front of the fort. The rugged Virginians and their French compatriots stood at attention in two long columns outside the main gate.

Sergeant Pierre Grimard occupied in his place of authority in the line of Vincennes militiamen. Little Pierre stood proudly to his father's left. Charles Rimbault and Francois Turpin stood to their sergeant's right. The other four members of the youthful ring of Vincennes spies stood in line beside their own fathers.

The sharp crack of a pistol signaled that the hour of surrender had arrived. Moments later a drum sounded a slow march from behind the gate. The doors swung open wide as Lieutenant Governor Henry Hamilton and Major Jehu Hay led the procession of defeated defenders. The red-coated soldiers of Great Britain followed behind their commanders. The French militia from Canada and a handful of Indians brought up the rear.

Little Pierre could not believe that he was taking part in such a historic event! He and his friends were all under ten years of age, yet they had each played an important part in the victory. They had gone on spy missions, rolled cartridges for the soldiers, and delivered supplies to the firing line. Pierre had even helped his father escape from the British jail!

Pierre worried that he might never again have such an amazing adventure. But still, he was so very proud to be a member of the Vincennes militia. Not many boys his age would ever have such exciting stories to tell. He and his friends had taken part in an important battle of the American Revolution! They had actually taken part in winning the freedom of the United States of America! They were proud citizens of a brand new nation.

Pierre was filled with emotion. He was so very proud of his spy friends and the men of Vincennes. He wanted to celebrate. He wanted to cheer! So, just as Governor Hamilton walked in front of him, Pierre reached up and removed his hat, and waved it high in the air. Then he shouted in his native French, *"Vive les États-Unis d'Amérique! Vive la liberté!"*

In English his words meant, "Long live the United States of America! Long live liberty!"

All of the people gathered outside the fort stared at him with bewildered looks. The British stopped marching and stared. The Virginia Long Knives stared. Even the Frenchmen of Vincennes stared at this spunky little French boy who had shouted such bold, patriotic words in the face of the fearsome Governor Hamilton.

Then, quite suddenly, both rows of the exhausted, filthy, proud Patriots erupted into wild cheers and a chorus of, "Huzzah! Huzzah! Huzzah!" They screamed and howled and waved their hats and muskets in the air.

The men standing close to Pierre patted his shoulders and rubbed his head. Pierre's father wrapped a proud arm around him and hugged him tight. Gaspard Turpin gave a huge wink. Little Pierre just stood and smiled his mischievous smile.

Governor Hamilton seemed to be very offended by the disrespectful little boy and all of the cheering. He thrust his chest out and held his chin high as he and Major Hay continued their march toward the awaiting Colonel George Rogers Clark.

After a long, humiliating walk they stopped two paces in front of the victorious officer. The drum cadence ceased. The enemy soldiers halted as both Hamilton and Hay dutifully removed their swords and presented them to the Colonel Clark.

"The fort is yours, Colonel," stated Hamilton flatly.

"The fort is mine, sir," responded Colonel Clark.

And just like that … it was over. Fort Sackville was once again Fort Patrick Henry. The British were defeated. Vincennes was, once again, free.

Vincennes, though only a tiny village on the remote frontier, would be forever remembered as an important battleground in the American Revolution. It was a great victory for the United States, for the people of the Illinois Country, and for the ***Little Spy of Vincennes*** and his courageous band of friends.

THE REAL PIERRE GRIMARD AND HIS FAMILY

Most of the characters in this story were real people. Pierre Grimard, Sr., was my wife's fifth great-grandfather. He was born in France and migrated to America in the 1760's. He married Genevieve Colomb in New Orleans in 1769 and then traveled up the Mississippi River to settle in the remote Illinois Country. He served in the Vincennes militia in 1778 and 1779 under Captain Bousseron and took part in the battle for Fort Sackville.

Pierre, Jr., and his brothers and sisters lived most of their lives in Vincennes and the towns nearby. My wife descends from Pierre's younger brother, Charles Grimard. Charles actually married one of the daughters of Francois and Josephine Turpin, which means that they are my wife's fifth great-grandparents, as well! She has two residents of Vincennes and French Patriots of the American Revolution in her family tree!

The elder Pierre Grimard died in 1784, just five years after the battle in Vincennes. Little Pierre was only fourteen years old at the time. We do not know how or why he died. He was buried in the cemetery beside the Old Cathedral Catholic Church in Vincennes, right next to the George Rogers Clark Memorial. That memorial sits on the exact site where Fort Sackville / Patrick Henry stood. You can actually see Pierre Grimard's military tombstone there if you ever have the chance to visit. (I included my own picture beside his headstone in the "About the Author" section.) If you ever get to visit the site, you will be standing on the exact spot where the battle of Fort Sackville took place!

If you have never been to Vincennes and experienced its rich heritage and history, I highly encourage you to do so. The best time to visit, in my opinion, is during the annual ***Spirit of Vincennes Rendezvous*** that takes place on Memorial Day weekend each May. Hundreds of Revolutionary War reenactors descend upon the little town of Vincennes and transform the area around the old Fort Sackville into an extensive 18th Century encampment. The weekend includes several battle reenactments, amazing food, wonderful shopping, and incredible hospitality. It is an awesome experience for kids. I hope to see you there next year! Come and visit with me at my book booth!

I hope that this story will help inspire you to explore you own personal history and find the exciting stories that lie undiscovered in your family tree. Though most of this book is fictional, it could very well have been the story of Pierre and the brave Grimard family. My desire is that their patriotism and sacrifices will never be forgotten.

Geoff Baggett

REVOLUTIONARY WAR GLOSSARY

Barracks – A form of housing or dormitory for soldiers. Their primary function was for sleeping. Often dozens of men were housed in these large buildings.

Bayonet – The sharp knife-like instrument that connects to the end of a military musket. It was used most often in hand-to-hand fighting.

Blockhouse – The corner structure that was usually included into the structure of the walls of a fort.

Breeches – These were the pants of the colonial period. They were secured with buttons and baggy in the seat. The pants reached just below the knee. Men typically wore long socks that covered their lower leg and extended up over the knee.

Brown Bess Musket – This is the name given to the British Army's military musket. They were mass-produced, smooth-barreled flintlock weapons that fired a .75 caliber (¾ inch) round lead ball.

Bullet / Ball / Musket Ball – The round lead balls fired from 18th century weapons.

Bullet Mold – Sized steel molds used to make rifle and musket projectiles. Melted lead was poured into these molds and allowed to cool, thus producing balls perfectly sized for weapons of the period.

Cannon – The artillery of Revolutionary War. These giant guns loaded through the muzzle and fired either large steel balls or clusters of steel or lead known as **grapeshot**.

Canteen – A receptacle used by soldiers to carry their personal supply of water.

Cartridge – These were pre-rolled ammunition packs for muskets. Made from paper, each cartridge resembled a stubby cigar, and contained the proper amount of gunpowder and a single lead projectile. Soldiers tore the cartridges open with their teeth, poured the gunpowder down the barrel of their weapon, and then rammed the paper and musket ball down the barrel.

Cease-Fire – A temporary stoppage of fighting, usually giving officers of opposing armies the opportunity to talk to one another under parley.

Charleville Musket – A French army musket that was common during the period of the American Revolution. It was a smooth-barreled flintlock weapon that fired a .69 caliber round lead ball.

Compatriots – Soldiers who fight alongside one another.

Continental Army – Soldiers in the federal army of the United States as authorized by the Continental Congress.

Crown – The shortened form of "**British Crown**." It was a reference to the form of British government, which was a kingdom. The king or queen was the wearer of the "crown."

Dragoons – A special type of soldier in the British army. They were "mounted infantry" who could either fight on horseback or on foot.

Earthworks – Piles of dirt, rock, and wood used as a barricade to protect soldiers from enemy gunfire. Soldiers often constructed these around their forts or around places that they were attacking.

Flintlock – The type of weapons, loaded through the muzzle, used during the American Revolution.

Fort Sackville – The name of the British fort/outpost at the village of Vincennes. When under the control of American forces, it was called Fort Patrick Henry.
Frizzen – The part of a flintlock weapon that the flint strikes to make a spark and ignite the gunpowder.
Gallows – Structures used for the execution of criminals by hanging.
Guardhouse – The jail inside a military facility.
Gunpowder – Also called "**powder**," this was an explosive compound that was used to fire weapons. Many men on the frontier carried their powder in hollowed out horns from bulls called, "**powder horns.**"
His Majesty – The proper, formal reference to the King of England. A queen is called, "Her Majesty."
Huzzah – A joyful shout, and the early form of the modern words "hoorah" and "hooray."
Indentured Servitude – This was a form of "voluntary slavery" in which poor people signed over their freedom to wealthy people for a set period of time. In return for their years of servitude they earned something such as passage by ship to America, the learning of a work trade, or shelter and food.
Indian – A traditional term used to refer to Native Americans. The term arose out of the confusion of early explorers. When they arrived in the Americas they thought that they had reached the east coast of India. Therefore, they referred to the native peoples as "Indians." The name "stuck" and became a word of common use in the United States.

Illinois Country – The common name of the entire region of modern-day Indiana and Illinois. Its westernmost border was the Mississippi River.
Injun – The slang word for "Indian."
Lead – The soft metal used to make projectiles for rifles and muskets. It is still used to make modern projectiles.
Leggings – Also known as "**Gaiters**," these were protective garments for the lower legs. They were often made of wool, canvas, cotton, or animal skins. They were secured with buttons or straps and served to protect and insulate the exposed lower leg between the breeches and shoes.
Litter – A makeshift vehicle used to transport sick or wounded soldiers. Similar to a modern stretcher, it was often made of cloth or animal skins suspended between two poles. It could be carried by people on foot or dragged behind a horse.
Long Knives – Recorded also as **Big Knives**, this was the name given by the local Native Americans to the Virginia Army under Col. George Rogers Clark.
Loyalist – A citizen of the American colonies loyal to King George III and Great Britain.
Militia – Local county and state military units. Most served locally. There were both Patriot and Loyalist militia units during the war. French militia units served with either the British or American forces.
Moccasins – Typical lightweight footwear of the Eastern Woodland Indians. Made from animal hides, these shoes often had a thread that was pulled through the leather on top that caused it to have its distinguishing "pucker."
Muster – The official forming of local militia units for mobilization in the war.

Oath of Allegiance – This was a custom in the 1700's. Men would "swear their oath" to a nation, state, or king as a demonstration of their loyalty. Men who swore such oaths usually signed their names on official documents. In the Revolutionary War this was a demonstration of Patriotic Service either to England or to the United States.

Palisades – Walls made from upright stakes or tree trunks that were often pointed on top. They were built for defense, such as in the walls of primitive forts.

Parley – Formal negotiations between opposing armies.

Patriots – People in American who were in favor of separation from England and the formation of a separate country.

Patrol – A military tactic which involved sending soldiers out into the countryside to scout for any presence of the enemy.

Queue – Pronounced "knew." This is the word for a man's ponytail. Men in Colonial times wore their hair long. They would often tie it in the back or braid it into a queue.

Redcoats – The derogatory name that Patriots called British soldiers.

Runner – Before the development of modern technology, messages had to be carried "on foot." Men or boys who delivered messages between a commander and the army were simply called "runners."

Spectacles – The old name for eyeglasses.

Shooting Pouch – A leather bag worn by frontiersmen. They carried their ammunition and tools for taking care of their musket or rifle in the pouch.

Siege – A military tactic in which an army surrounds another army, usually confined in a town or fort. Once the enemy army is contained, the army laying siege bombards them with fire until the army under siege calls for a surrender.

Station – Another name for a frontier fort.

Surrender – The formal, official end of a military conflict when one army acknowledges that the other is victor. Surrender often has certain terms to which both parties in the negotiation must agree.

Tomahawk – A bladed weapon that resembled an axe or hatchet. This useful tool was used both in combat as well as in camp life.

Tory / Tories – Another name for Loyalists.

Wax Seal – People usually sealed their private letters with a melted blob of hot wax and then pressed a piece of metal into the wax to make an impression or "seal." This was a way to ensure that private letters were not opened until they reached their destination.

Weskit – Also known as a **waistcoat**, this was the vest worn over the top of a man's shirt and under a man's coat. It would sometimes be worn without the outer overcoat. It was a more formal outer garment.

THANK YOU FOR READING MY STORY!

I hope that you enjoyed my work of fiction. It was a pleasure preparing and writing it for you. I am just a simple "part-time" author, and I am humbled that you chose to read my book.

I would humbly ask that you help me spread the word about my historical fiction books for kids. You can help me in a number of ways!

- **Tell your friends!** Word of mouth is always the best!
- **Mention my books on Facebook or in other social media.** I know lots of students use social media these days. Please mention me, or maybe even post a picture of you reading one of my books!
- **Get your parents to write a review for me on Amazon.com.** Reviews are so very important. They help other readers discover good books. Tell your parents what you thought about the book and ask them to put your words into the review.
- **Connect with me and like my author page on Facebook @cockedhatpublishing, and follow me on Twitter @GeoffBaggett.**
- **Tell your teachers about me!** I have a unique and interesting Revolutionary War presentation available for elementary and middle school classes. I actually bring a trunk full of items from the American Revolution and provide a "hands-on" experience for students. I even dress up couple of volunteers in replica Revolutionary War militia uniforms! I am a professional speaker and living historian, and I absolutely love to travel and visit in schools. Get your teachers to contact me through my web site, geoffbaggett.com, or through my Facebook author page, to arrange an event.

Thanks again! And remember to tell all of your friends about the Patriot Kids of the American Revolution Series!

Geoff Baggett

ABOUT THE AUTHOR

Geoff Baggett is a small-town pastor in rural Kentucky. Though his formal education and degrees are in the fields of chemistry, biology, and Christian theology, his hobbies and obsessions (according to his wife) are genealogy and Revolutionary War history. He is an active member of the Sons of the American Revolution and has discovered over twenty Patriot ancestors in his family tree from the states of Virginia, North and South Carolina, and Georgia.

Geoff is an avid living historian, appearing regularly in period uniform in classrooms, reenactments, and other Revolutionary War commemorative events throughout the southeastern United States. He lives on a small piece of land in rural Trigg County, Kentucky, with his amazing wife, a daughter and grandson, and a yard full of fruit trees and perpetually hungry chickens and goats.

Made in the USA
Columbia, SC
05 November 2017